Slices Of Life

A Novella

GEORGIA BEERS

SLICES OF LIFE

© 2012 BY GEORGIA BEERS

ISBN (10) 0-983-27584-X
ISBN (13) 978-0-98327584-8

THIS TRADE PAPERBACK ORIGINAL IS PUBLISHED BY BRISK PRESS, BRIELLE NEW JERSEY. 08730
EDITED BY LINDA LORENZO
COVER DESIGN AND LAYOUT BY STEFF OBKIRCHNER

FIRST PRINTING: OCTOBER 2012

By Georgia Beers

Novels

Finding Home
Mine
Fresh Tracks
Too Close to Touch
Thy Neighbor's Wife
Turning the Page
96 Hours
Slices of Life

Anthologies

Outsiders

Georgia Beers
www.georgiabeers.com

Acknowledgements

When I started writing this novella, I made the mistake of thinking that a collection of short stories would be easier to write than a novel, that it would zip along quickly. Oh, how wrong I was! Jumping in and out of the lives of eleven different characters was infinitely more difficult than I expected. So, as you can imagine, this book is a bit of a departure from my usual work, and I appreciate the patience and encouragement all of you showed. My readers are the best. I hope I don't let you down.

Thank you to Susan and Carrie at Brisk Press for being the easiest, most laid-back people on the planet to work with. When I told them this was going to end up being a novella rather than a full-length novel, they didn't bat an eye. They just said, "Okay, let's do it." And just like that, you're reading it.

One of the biggest mistakes an author can make—in my opinion—is to think she has nothing left to learn about her craft. Linda Lorenzo edited this book with a gentle hand, explaining each correction to me in detail, helping me to understand and learn to make the proper changes to my work. I was a good English student in school, and in my forties, I'm still learning. For that, I am eternally grateful.

My dearest friend, Steff Obkirchner, never ceases to amaze me with her artistic abilities. Not only is she my most amazing proofreader (or Queen Nitpicker, as I like to call her), but she also designed both the cover and the trailer for this collection. I owe her big.

I've never been a part of a writers group before. I never wanted to be. I always thought having a group of people evaluate my work would do nothing but depress me, so I avoided it. But since my group started meeting a year ago, I realize how wonderful and important it is to spend time with like-minded people. So thank you to my Cool

Chicks: Joy, Nancy, Tracy, Jess, and Karin. Your support means everything.

Finally, but never last, my Bonnie. I am not the easiest person to be partners with (hard to believe, I know). I can be selfish, moody, insecure, solitary, and just difficult in general. But Bonnie knows all of this about me, understands it all, and she loves me anyway. Becoming instant parents to a teenager is enough to throw anyone's life into chaos, and ours was no different. In the process, we've found some interesting things out about ourselves and each other—both good and bad. We've argued. We've disagreed on how to handle things. We've had moments of bliss when we've realized we did something exactly right. It's been an emotional rollercoaster, but through it all, we've tried our best to stand together, and I think we're doing a damn good job. Thank you, my love, not only for your unconditional support of my career, but for sticking with me through the good and the bad, the annoying and the awesome, the heartache and the elation. I know I don't always make it easy, but I'm so glad to have you standing solidly by my side, holding my hand. I love you.

THE ADMINISTRATIVE ASSISTANT

Acting like some kind of weird atmospheric vacuum, the navy-blue pinstripe pantsuit sucked all the breathable air out of the room. Jenna could feel her own struggle for oxygen as Christine Davis breezed in like she owned the place—she did—and carried herself as if no other woman could look quite as stunning in that navy-blue pinstripe pantsuit. Probably true.

"Ms. Buckner," she said absently to Jenna as she retrieved her messages from the little turnstile on the counter. "Good morning."

"Good morning, Ms. Davis," Jenna replied, equally nonchalant.

"We've got Sal Farelli and his crew coming in at nine thirty. Please make sure we have fresh coffee and pastries in the conference room before then."

"Yes, ma'am."

Davis didn't look up from the pink message slips in her hand as she headed down the hall toward her enormous and expensively appointed corner office. Jenna's eyes followed her retreat, glued to the gentle swaying of slim hips and the sharp cut of a set of calf muscles that were very, very well acquainted with a bicycle.

"God help me," she muttered under her breath.

"God thinks you're a hopeless case." Roberta McKenzie—Bertie to most—shared the Davis and Fichter, Attorneys-at-Law front-desk area with Jenna. She locked her purse in the bottom drawer, set a medium double-double coffee from Tim Horton's in front of Jenna, then plopped into her chair, donned her headset, and patted her carrot-top hair into place. She sipped from her own cup before she continued. "How many times do I have to remind you that lusting after your boss gets you nowhere? Hmm?"

"Apparently, a few more."

"Were you this stubborn in grade school too?"

"You'll have to ask my mom."

"Okay, let's try again." Bertie ticked off her points on her fingers. "It's inappropriate, for starters."

"Yeah, yeah. I know."

"Secondly, it distracts you from your work."

Jenna furrowed her brow. "You think so? I might have to disagree with that one." She was totally playing with Bertie now.

"All right. How about the fact that she's taken." Jenna made a face and gave a dismissive wave. Bertie glared for a second, then went on. "Oh, yeah, and there's the whole thing about it being *inappropriate.*"

Jenna laughed at that. "But have you *seen* her?"

"I have. She does nothing for me."

"Spoken like a true straight woman."

It was Bertie's turn to laugh as she clicked open her e-mail. "Seriously, hon. You can look, but you can't touch."

"Yes, Oh Wise One," Jenna said, as if she hadn't already touched. As if she hadn't been touching every Tuesday and Thursday night for the past two months. As if Christine Davis's head wasn't snug between Jenna's thighs a mere eight hours ago. She glanced at Bertie, half-expecting her to see the aura of guilt that must surround Jenna's entire form. What color was guilt anyway? Black? Red? But Bertie continued on with her e-mail and Jenna was apparently aura-less.

Nobody knew. Nobody. Not Jenna's best friend, Michelle. Not her parents. Nobody at the office. Not a soul. Christine wanted it that way, said it was safer. Jenna was too preoccupied with the mind-blowing sex to stop and ask the obvious question: Safer for whom?

Mind-blowing. That wasn't even a strong enough description. Earth-shattering, maybe? Limb-melting? Jenna hated to think of herself as the kind of person who had a one-track mind, but when she was alone with Christine, her hormones went whacky. All she could think about was stripping her clothes off and letting Christine have her way with her body. All other coherent thought seemed to flee from her brain.

Christine Davis wasn't conventionally pretty. She was actually rather plain, with the exception of her eyes. Her straight, brown hair was cut simply in a short, practical bob which she tucked behind her ears by habit. Her skin was clear and smooth and generally devoid of makeup. But her eyes were ice blue, such a light shade that they almost seemed clear, at times nearly transparent. When Christine Davis looked directly at you, she could make you squirm purely because of the color of her eyes.

But it wasn't really her physical appearance that entranced Jenna. It was her poise. Her confidence. The certainty that she would get whatever she wanted whenever she wanted it. Jenna imagined that there wasn't a lot in life Christine Davis longed for, and she'd found herself attracted to her from almost the minute she was hired over a year ago.

At some point last month, Christine decided she wanted Jenna. To Jenna, it was unclear what changed, what made her boss suddenly look at her differently. But it didn't take much for Christine to convince Jenna their pairing was a good idea. One late night at work, one glass of wine too many, one soul-searing kiss. That was all it took; Jenna was on her back on the leather couch in Christine's office in no time, her skirt hiked up around her hips, her panties dangling from one ankle, and her boss's fingers deep inside her. She wasn't sure if it was the risk of being in the workplace while the cleaning staff was still there, having sex with the woman she'd lusted over for months and months, or having Christine's hand clamped over her mouth to muffle her cries, but Jenna came harder than she ever had before. It was the most massive, spine-sizzling orgasm of her life; she was completely useless afterward. Her limbs felt like Jell-O, her vision was blurred, and she couldn't feel her feet.

"My, my. That was *nice*." Christine kissed her gently on the mouth, then the forehead, before extracting herself from their tangle and standing up.

All Jenna could do was nod and watch as Christine straightened her blouse and stepped back into her shoes.

"Thank you for indulging me. Maybe we can do it again?"

It wasn't really a question and Jenna didn't stop to analyze the thank you. Her eyes closed, she simply gave another nod.

"Hey." Christine's voice was gentle as her fingers brushed Jenna's hair off her face. "Don't fall asleep here. It's time to go home."

"'Kay." Jenna took the hand Christine held out and let her pull her to her feet. There wasn't much talking after that. They packed up their things and rode the elevator down to the lobby of the building together. Christine said goodnight, that she'd see Jenna in the morning, and that was that.

Until the next time, less than a week later.

After that, it became their routine. By their third time, the discussion of keeping the situation just between the two of them came up, and before Jenna could think clearly, she'd become, for all intents and purposes, Christine's little concubine.

She would have been disgusted with herself if the sex wasn't so goddamn good. At least, that's how she felt in the beginning.

The phone on her desk rang, snapping her back to the present.

"Davis and Fichter. How may I help you?" Jenna absently wondered how many times a day she said those words. Dozens, at the very least.

"Hi, Jenna. It's Jules. How are you this morning, hon?"

Jenna's stomach roiled and her coffee suddenly felt like acid. *Why did she always have to be so nice? Why couldn't she just be a bitch?* These thoughts raced through her head every time Christine's partner of over a decade called, every time she asked Jenna about her life or her family. Jules was a sweetheart. Jenna hated her for that.

"I'm fine. How are you?"

"I'd be better if my lovely wife would answer her cell phone when I call." She feigned annoyance, but if there was one thing Jenna learned about Jules during the time she'd worked for Christine, it was that the woman was perpetually cheerful. "Is she in?"

"She is. Let me buzz her for you." Jenna was shocked to see a slight tremble in her hand as she put Jules on hold and dialed Christine's extension.

"Ms. Davis?"

"Yes?"

"Jules is on line three."

"Oh! Great." Christine sounded genuinely happy to hear from her partner. "Put her through."

Jenna did so, her hand still quivering. *What the hell is wrong with me?* She flexed her fingers, opened and closed her hand until the tremor stopped.

"Everything okay?" Bertie asked, arching an eyebrow.

"Yeah. Fine."

Bertie continued looking at her even as she spoke into the small microphone of her headset, apparently answering a question posed to her.

Jenna gave her a look that said, "What?" Bertie turned back to her computer while Jenna wondered what that was about.

A glance at her switchboard told her Jules and Christine were still talking. Jenna wasn't sure why that suddenly made her uncomfortable, but she squirmed in her ergonomic office chair and wondered if she wasn't coming down with something. Her stomach still felt off, her body was restless, and a slow tension was building in her head as if her skull was in a gradually tightening, padded vice. A deep breath in and then gradually out seemed to steady her somewhat as she tried to relax and put her own mind at ease.

She was still staring off into space when the elevator across from the double glass doors to the hall dinged, and Kerry St. John stepped out with two boxes of doughnuts stacked in her arms. Shifting them to one arm, she opened the door with the other before Jenna or Bertie could get up and open it for her. Kerry was their new intern. Their tall, blonde, young, legs-that-went-on-for-days intern. She was always smiling, always cheerful, and—Jenna suspected—playing the dumb-blonde card on purpose. The men in the office fell all over themselves to help/teach/talk to/look at her. Jenna and Bertie just rolled their eyes over such displays.

"Hey there." Christine's voice snagged Jenna's attention, but as she turned and tried to dim the wattage on her smile, she realized that Christine wasn't talking to her. She was talking to Kerry.

"Hi, Boss," Kerry said, her tone so saccharine and kind that Jenna wanted to lunge across the counter, grab her by the throat, and shake the sugar right out of her. "I come bearing gifts for the meeting."

"I see that. Excellent." Christine laid a hand on the small of Kerry's back. "Walk with me to the conference room." Then over her shoulder, she tossed, "Jenna, is the coffee ready?"

Jenna's nostrils flared as she watched the two women head down the hall, walking entirely too close together as far as she was concerned. An ache in her jaw became noticeable; only then did she realize she was clenching her teeth together as hard as possible.

"What do you think she's on?" Bertie whispered.

Jenna blinked several times and turned to look at her friend. "What?"

"Kerry. Nobody's *that* happy *all* the time. She's got to be on something. I wonder what it is. I wonder where I can get some."

That small bit of Bertie's humor broke some of the tension for Jenna, allowed her to take a deep breath and stop worrying about suddenly feeling so weirdly insecure. At least for a while.

Focusing on work was the best thing for her and Jenna knew it. She got the coffee brewed and stocked the conference room with the fresh pot, clean black mugs with the Davis & Fichter logo printed on them in gold, spoons, sugar, creamer, napkins, and tea bags. Then she took Kerry's stupid doughnuts and arranged them tastefully on a round plate, all the while shaking her head in disapproval. Didn't the intern know how tacky it looked to serve clients pastries from a box?

When the room looked distinguished and presentable, Jenna stepped into the burgundy-carpeted hallway. She was just in time to see Christine's office door open. Christine and Kerry lingered in the doorway, apparently finishing whatever conversation started inside. Christine said something Jenna couldn't make out and Kerry laughed, a high-pitched tinkling sound that made Jenna cringe. Kerry laid her hand on Christine's shoulder and leaned in close to respond. Then she turned and headed down the hall to the left. Christine stood in her doorway and watched her intern saunter away before retreating to her office. Neither of them noticed Jenna watching.

Not wanting to analyze why the scene bothered her, but unable to think about anything else, Jenna swallowed the lump in her throat. What was the big deal? Yes, she was sleeping with Christine, but she was by no means in love with her. *Right?* It was just sex. *Wasn't it?* In the beginning, she didn't think of Christine as any kind of predator. True, she was the boss and the boss shouldn't be sleeping with her subordinate, but Jenna was just as guilty. She wanted it just as much;

Christine certainly didn't force her. But after what she just witnessed, the whole bit about secrecy began to make sense. It never once occurred to Jenna that she wasn't the only one in the office Christine bedded or intended to bed, and the scope of her naïveté was suddenly, acutely embarrassing. She wasn't sixteen. She was a grown woman. A grown woman who should have known better.

Now, as she flopped back down into her chair, Jenna wondered which of them was the bigger cliché—her for banging her boss or Christine for banging her secretary. Both were equally unimpressive.

Before she could wallow further in her own self-deprecation, the door opened and Sal Farelli entered, flanked by three men and a woman. Farelli owned six car dealerships in the area and was, by far, one of the most successful businessmen in the city. Everybody knew his name because of his wealth. Everybody knew his face because of his television commercials.

Jenna didn't like Farelli and her conclusion was based simply on the way he presented himself. Most of Christine's clients were average businesspeople, but Sal Farelli was a caricature of a middle-aged, Italian male. Of average height, he had a squat build and a bit of a gut. He was in his mid-fifties, and his salt-and-pepper hair was slicked back, giving him the stereotypical greasy look of a car salesman. He wore jeans, a black and white bowling shirt, and sunglasses. He looked like he had come directly from the set of *The Sopranos*, and Jenna often wondered if he was in some sort of mafia. Her next thought was that he was a walking cliché, which brought a bit of a grin to her face until she remembered that she also fit that category.

"Hiya, doll," he said to her, removing his sunglasses and grinning at her as if expecting her to swoon. Jenna had to fight to keep from rolling her eyes.

In the end, she ironically decided she was almost grateful for Farelli's appointment because it kept her mind off her situation with Christine. Kerry the Intern got to sit in on the meeting, much to Farelli's delight, and Jenna was very happy to close the door on them and walk back to her desk. She didn't think she could handle the way everybody in the room leered at Kerry, Christine included.

"You okay?" Bertie asked her as she sat back down in her chair and tried to focus on her computer. "You seem tense."

"I'm fine," Jenna told her. "Tired, I guess."

Bertie gave a nod and they each went back to their work.

A few minutes later, Jenna spoke again. "Bertie?"

"Hmm?"

"Have you ever done anything that you regretted later? Something you thought was a good idea at the time, but turned out not to be?"

"Such as?"

Jenna sighed, frustrated with herself for bringing it up. She wanted somebody with whom to commiserate, but didn't want to reveal what she'd been up to. "I don't know. Dating somebody for the wrong reasons. Something like that?"

Bertie chuckled. "Dating somebody. Sleeping with somebody. Oh, yeah. Who hasn't?"

Jenna chuckled too, not wanting to seem overly serious. "Right? Yeah, my sister has been seeing somebody she knows she shouldn't be seeing, but isn't sure how to get out of it."

"Does she want to get out of it?"

Jenna cocked her head, contemplating the question, and answered in a voice much softer than she intended. "Yeah, I think she does."

"The sex must be good." Bertie shot her a knowing grin.

"She says it's incredible."

Bertie nodded, her eyes on her computer screen. "That's what usually keeps 'em hanging on."

"I'm just not sure what to tell her," Jenna pressed gently. Bertie was older, wiser, and no-nonsense. Jenna wanted very much to get direction from her.

"Tell her she already knows what she should do. She's just ignoring her instincts."

"Yeah. You're probably right." Jenna chewed on that for the next hour, knowing deep down that Bertie was right. *I am sleeping with my boss. I am a living, breathing Lifetime movie.* She closed her eyes and shook her head, horribly dismayed with the decisions she'd made, and utterly disgusted by the fact that she'd become "the other woman." Her feminist friends would skin her alive if they knew.

By eleven o'clock, Jenna succeeded in focusing the majority of her attention on her work, which gave her brain a much-needed respite. Rolling a terrible judgment call around in your head over and over again can be exhausting; attempting to come up with the best way to fix it, even more so. Jenna was very happy to work on some invoicing, send out statements to overdue clients, and prepare the outgoing mail. Busywork became her savior and she was grateful.

Just before 11:30, the elevator door opened and a compact, yet muscular, woman exited, pulling a cart of packages behind her. Leaving her cart in the hall, she entered the office. She was dressed in brown from head to toe, her dark hair was close-cropped with gray sprinkling the temples, and her smile was contagious.

"Hey there, good lookin'," she said to Jenna as she set three small boxes and four envelopes on the counter.

"Good morning, MJ," Jenna replied. "How are you today?"

"Can't complain" was MJ's stock answer, every day, no matter what. She scanned each package with her UPS computer board, then gave the board to Jenna, along with the plastic pen for her signature.

"Well, you *could*," Jenna said with a grin.

"But what good would it do me?" MJ winked.

"She has a point," Bertie piped in.

Jenna sighed as she signed on the little computer screen, her writing nearly illegible. "I know."

MJ leaned on her forearms, pushing herself closer to Jenna. "Hey," she said, her voice soft. "Don't let the assholes of the world get you down. You deserve better. Okay?" She held Jenna's gaze with her own, and Jenna marveled at the lushness of her dark eyelashes, devoid of any makeup and in no need of it. Her dark skin was nearly flawless, causing Jenna to wonder if it was as soft as it looked.

"Okay," Jenna said with a nod, handing the computer board back. "Thanks, MJ."

MJ ran a hand over the top of her head and Jenna had the sudden urge to do the same thing. "My pleasure. Have a great day. See you tomorrow."

"You too."

Jenna and Bertie both watched as MJ left their office and took her cart off to the next business on their floor.

"That one is a charmer," Bertie said with a chuckle. "She even gives me a tingle. Don't tell my husband."

Jenna nodded, her eyes still on the empty hall.

"See? Why can't you lust after somebody like that?" Bertie asked. "She's intelligent, she works hard, she's perceptive, she's adorable. You like her. And I think she's got a little crush on you."

Jenna continued to nod. Bertie was right. From the first day MJ took over this route, she and Jenna clicked. Jenna didn't know if it was their gaydar or a mutual attraction or both, but she always got a bit of a flutter in her belly whenever MJ came through the door. And MJ always made sure to stop and chat with her, even if it was only for a moment or two, no matter how busy she was. She always paid Jenna some kind of compliment, no matter how small, and by the time MJ left the office, Jenna seemed to feel a bit better, a bit lighter. It was funny how a five-minute visit from somebody could change the very atmosphere you sat in. MJ had that effect. In fact, Jenna was toying with the idea of asking MJ out for coffee.

Then the fateful after-hours meeting with Christine happened and all bets were off. *Stupid, stupid, stupid.*

"Really," Bertie was saying. "You two would make such a cute couple and I bet she'd treat you like a queen. I wonder if she's available."

Jenna wondered, too.

She worked through lunch, her brain half on her work and half on her UPS driver. More than once, she caught herself smiling for no reason and it was such a new feeling. The idea of thinking about somebody she could openly discuss seemed almost foreign. Funny how that happened in less than two months, how having a secret affair made her feel so closed, so alone, so…not a good person.

What she was doing with Christine was wrong. She knew that from the beginning, but now it made her almost nauseous. Yes, the sex was fantastic. So what? Christine was spoken for. She knew it and Jenna knew it. For the first time, she allowed herself to think about how it would feel to be in Jules' shoes, what it would do to her trust, her self-worth, her heart, if she knew the person she loved was being intimate with somebody else and hiding it from her. If that other person was somebody she knew, somebody who smiled and said hello and pretended to be a friend, all the while knowing full well she was stabbing her in the back. Jenna's stomach churned and she tasted bile in the back of her throat.

"Hey, what's going on with you today?" Bertie asked with concern. "You look almost green, hon."

Jenna swallowed hard. "I don't feel so good."

"I can tell. Look, it's after two. Why don't you just go home? You worked through lunch and you're caught up, right?"

Jenna nodded.

"I'll cover your phones. Just go."

"You're sure?"

"I'm sure I don't want to clean your puke up off the desk." Bertie's grin took any snark out of the comment.

"All right." Jenna quickly packed up her things. Despite the upset stomach, she'd made a decision and she felt good about it. She may not be the only woman Christine was—or would be—having an affair with, but she could put a stop to her participation in it. She felt she owed Jules a big apology, but it wasn't her place to reveal Christine's dalliances. That was between the two partners and Jenna hoped that it wouldn't be long before all was revealed. It would hurt Jules, that was certain, but in the long run, it would be better for her to know.

Wouldn't it?

She shook the thought from her head. It was too much for her right now. She just wanted to get out of the office where Christine was. It was suddenly stifling and she had trouble taking in air.

"Go home, drink some fluids, and get some rest," Bertie was saying as Jenna grabbed her jacket and slung her shoulder bag over her arm.

"Yes, ma'am. Thanks, Bertie."

"No problem." The phone rang. "I've got it. Go."

Jenna headed for the door.

"Good afternoon, Davis and Fichter. How may I help you?" Bertie said behind her. "Oh, hello, Mr. Conrad…"

On her way past the chairs in the waiting area, Jenna grabbed a copy of the day's paper.

The last person who'd read it left the Help Wanted section on top.

THE UPS DRIVER

Mary Jane Harter wasn't quite certain of the name of the tune stuck in her head, but she whistled it anyway as she pulled her van around and behind the little strip mall. Four deliveries here, one across the street, business pick-ups, and then she'd start on her residential deliveries, which she always did last.

MJ— nobody called her by her given name other than her mother and then only when she was angry—loved her job. It was hard work, both physically and mentally, especially around the holiday season, but she loved the challenge. It took organization, timing, muscle, and people skills didn't hurt. She liked that she did her job alone, but got to chat a little bit with dozens of different people a day.

The early fall afternoon was gorgeous. Sunny, not too hot, not too cool. MJ loaded up her wheeled cart, deciding she had the time to walk the deliveries rather than drive from loading dock to loading dock. The strip mall was small enough and her load wasn't huge; the fresh air felt good as it filled her lungs.

"Hey, MJ." The young man at the Verizon store was cute, in a nerdy kind of way. His skinny body clothed in dress slacks, an oxford, and a tie, gave him the look of a boy trying on his dad's work clothes.

"Hi, Danny. How's school?" MJ handed over her computer board. "Just three for you today."

Danny took the board and signed his name as he said, "School is…hard."

"I think that's the feeling of many a college freshman. You hang in there. It's good for you. It'll be worth it."

"That's what I keep telling myself."

"Take it from somebody who didn't go to college, but wishes she had. You work hard and keep the faith."

"I will. Thanks, MJ."

Still whistling the nameless tune, MJ moved on down the line to the next shop, a General Nutrition Center. GNC always made her pause and wonder at all the powders, pills, supplements, and energy food. It also made her wonder if she should look more carefully at some of it.

She loved her job, it was true, but she was fast approaching middle age and, much as she hated to admit it, she wasn't going to be able to haul fifty-pound packages up and down stairs for all that much longer. She enjoyed it now, but it was becoming a common occurrence to end up icing her knee or soaking in a hot, epsom-salt bath at the end of the day to ease the ache in her back. She worked out regularly with the free weights in her basement, and she considered herself a stronger-than-average woman. Hell, she had to be to compete with the men in her line of work. But age wasn't something she could fight, and trying not to think about it didn't change anything.

Of course, once she began thinking about aging, her single status came screeching to the forefront. She'd always been perfectly happy being on her own, hooking up with an occasional woman here and there, having some fun, some recreational sex, but nothing permanent. No, she was too independent, too set in her ways to settle down. Besides, what good was it to have somebody you called family? Hers had taught her how unreliable they could be when they tossed her out at age seventeen because she told them about her sexuality. Her mother had since come around, and they now had occasional visits, lunches or dinners together a couple of times a month, but she had not spoken a word to her father in nearly thirty years. As far as he was concerned, she'd given him the worst possible news she could, and she no longer existed in his eyes.

At first, MJ was totally crushed by her father's condemnation of her. He was a church-going, African-American man who'd worked hard his whole life, and for him to consider his only daughter a blight on his otherwise spotless record hurt her like nothing MJ could ever imagine. She tried for weeks to redeem herself, going so far as to contemplate recanting, denying her true self in order to win back his love. She even made the mistake of trying to reason with him, telling him she didn't understand how he could be part of a race that was, and still is, continually discriminated against, but then turn around and discriminate against another group.

That argument only enraged him, and he gave her a twenty-minute-long diatribe about how she could hide her sexuality, but he couldn't hide his skin color and *how dare she* compare the two. MJ was utterly confused by his logic. So, because she could hide her true self, it was okay for people to discriminate against her, but because he couldn't hide his, it wasn't? That made no sense to her and she told him so…which turned out to be a mistake because it earned her nothing from him but a crack in the mouth. Certainly not the first one, but most definitely the last.

It was her mother who brought her back to her senses. She could still hear her words, spoken in hushed tones, but filled with such passion: *Don't you let him dictate who you are, MJ. You're a good girl and you're who God made you to be. Your father doesn't get to judge what's right and wrong, he just thinks he does. If he wants to be a fool, you let him be a fool. He'll regret it one day.*

MJ was still waiting for "one day," but it hadn't arrived yet.

So she took her mother's advice and went on with her life, dating women, taking them home, moving on to the next. She carefully—and somewhat unconsciously, she now realized—made sure not to bring anybody else into her life who might end up tossing her aside like old sneakers the way her father had. But now, as she approached fifty, MJ was acutely aware of the problem created by insulating herself from the pain others might cause: an unrelenting loneliness.

It bothered her that she was lonely.

It bothered her a lot.

And that thought brought an image of Jenna Buckner to her mind.

MJ didn't make it a habit of fantasizing about her clientele. Truth be told, a lot of them looked at her as beneath them. After all, she was a simple UPS delivery person, a necessity, like a janitor or a mailman. She had customers who barely made eye contact with her when she dropped off a package. But Jenna...she was sweet and kind. And friendly. And very, *very* cute. MJ often rolled around in her head the idea of asking her out. She just wasn't sure how she should go about it. And what if she said no? God, what if she wasn't even gay? Though she did ping MJ's gaydar in a pretty significant way. Deliveries to Davis & Fichter would become unendingly awkward. Maybe she was better off just staying single. Maybe.

Shaking off the melancholy that threatened to overtake her thoughts, she tried to focus on the rest of her day and got in and out of GNC without asking the clerk what sorts of products he'd recommend for an aging, physically active person whose job involved lots of lifting.

The weather stayed blissful and MJ was able to relax and do her job. It was a quality she really liked about herself: the ability to compartmentalize her feelings, put the annoying or distracting ones on a shelf for later, and get on with her work. Once she'd delivered all the business packages, she did her business pick-ups and then focused on her residential deliveries.

The customers who received deliveries at home were an entirely different breed than the offices she delivered to between nine and five. Some were people who worked from home. Some were stay-at-home moms or dads who purchased something online or off the television. Some items were gifts. Some were necessities. But regardless, the recipients were almost always friendlier, more relaxed, and less frazzled than the people she saw during business hours. Residential deliveries were MJ's favorites.

She hit three in a row that were people who "telecommuted." This was a fairly new prospect to MJ. Sort of like working from home, yet not for yourself. These people worked for actual businesses, got deliveries from the main office, but did whatever they did from the comfort of their own homes, often unshowered and in their pajamas. MJ knew this was incredibly appealing to a lot of people, but she didn't think she could do it. She liked to get out, to see the world. She needed to commune with people during her day. Sitting home alone for eight hours nonstop would drive her insane.

Kevin Herkle was a big guy, both in height and in girth. He answered the door, as he always did, wearing sweatpants and a ratty T-shirt. Today's shirt had an Adidas logo so faded it was almost impossible to read. He blinked in the sunlight like a man emerging from a darkened cave.

"Hey, MJ. Sun's out," he said needlessly.

"Sure is," MJ replied, handing over his package.

"Wow. Nice day."

"You need a window office, Kevin."

"Too distracting," he said as he signed. "If I can see outside, I'll want to *be* outside. Can't work outside. It's better not to look."

"Understood. Hang in there."

"You too."

Her knocks going unanswered, she left two packages at two different side doors, and continued to whistle the same unnamable tune as she maneuvered her van through the narrow streets of the neighborhood. People out working in their yards waved to her, and she thought again how much she enjoyed her job. Oh, sure, there were company issues and dumb rules and too much politics involved as far as she was concerned. But in the grand scheme of things, she had a job she didn't hate, she had good benefits, and she made a good buck. All in all, not a bad deal.

MJ pulled up at the curb in front of 217 Magnolia and cut the ignition. It was a large, classy house with impeccable landscaping and lush green grass. Sometimes, MJ liked to play little guessing games, trying to see if she could figure out the story of the recipient of her deliveries. For example, Sarah Holt received deliveries on a fairly regular basis and was almost always home to sign for them. The shippers covered a wide range of products and subjects: Zappos, Amazon, LL Bean, JC Penney, Gap for Kids. Given the smattering of toys in the driveway and the fact that she tended to answer the door with a child of no more than two on her hip, MJ's obvious conclusion was that Sarah Holt was a stay-at-home mom.

MJ rang the doorbell and edited her conclusion when the door was opened.

"Hi there, MJ."

Sarah Holt was a *very hot*, stay-at-home mom.

Blonde curls pulled back into a ponytail, she wore simple cutoff shorts that accentuated legs that were long and shapely and seemed too perfect to even be real. Her long-sleeve T-shirt was femininely cut and gym-class gray, and she had the sleeves pulled up to mid-forearm. MJ had to consciously keep her eyes focused straight ahead so she wouldn't be tempted to follow the dip in the V-neck. The toddler was perched on her hip like an accessory. She was quiet today with her head on Sarah's shoulder, her thumb in her mouth, and her big blue eyes that were carbon copies of Sarah's staring unblinkingly at MJ.

"Got three for you today, Mrs. Holt," MJ said politely as she handed over the computer for a signature and winked at the baby.

Sarah stopped with the pen in mid-air. "I'm sorry. What did you call me?"

MJ laughed. "Sarah. I meant to say Sarah."

"That's what I thought." Over her shoulder, she called out, "Rebecca, would you grab a bottle of water out of the fridge for MJ?"

"You don't have to do that," MJ protested.

"Unless you'd rather have a beer..." Sarah blinked those big blue eyes in mock innocence and MJ couldn't help but chuckle.

"Much as I'd love to, it's probably not a good idea."

A sigh. "I suppose you're right. Water it is, then."

"Ask and you shall receive." Rebecca Martin, tall and willowy with chestnut hair and a dimpled chin, handed a bottle over to MJ. She was slightly taller than Sarah and lived four houses down. MJ had met her on several occasions when she had something to deliver. She seemed to spend a lot of time at Sarah's, and MJ predicted she was a stay-at-home mom too. MJ wondered if their kids were the same ages, if they were best friends, what their connection might be.

"What'd you get?" Rebecca asked peering over Sarah's shoulder at the boxes.

"Nothing exciting, I'm afraid. A winter coat for Jeremy—the sleeves on his old one don't even cover his wrists anymore. God, he's growing like a weed—some sneakers for Jessie."

"What's in the third box?"

"Oh. It's, um, just some books." An off-hand shrug.

Rebecca rolled her eyes. "Bo-ring! Anything livelier on that truck of yours, MJ?"

"It's a pretty tame load today, sorry to say."

"Ugh! Damn suburbs." She waved a hand dismissively and went back into the house and out of sight.

Sarah shook her head with a grin and handed MJ her computer board. "Almost done?"

"Maybe a dozen more stops. Fifteen. Not many."

"Nice day for it."

"Sure is. You have yourself a great evening, Sarah."

"You too, MJ."

The UPS van coughed to a start and MJ gave a wave and a short horn toot to Sarah as she pulled away. Yes, that Mr. Holt was one lucky guy. Somehow that brought her thoughts back around to Jenna Buckner at Davis and Fichter. What would it hurt to ask her out? Just something neutral, like coffee, just to see what they might have in common. It could be a little awkward, but what attempt at asking for a date wasn't? Awkward was just part of the deal, right? MJ was a big girl; she could handle it. Life was too short to sit around wondering if you should have tried something, said something, done something.

She wasn't one for sitting around.

Tomorrow, she would do it. She'd ask Jenna to coffee.

Tomorrow.

The nameless tune came back to her lips and she whistled away the rest of her route.

"Do you think she wishes she was a guy?" Rebecca asked as Sarah closed the front door.

"Who? MJ? Why would she wish that?"

Rebecca lifted one shoulder. "I don't know. I mean, she's got to be a lesbian, right?"

"Why do you say that?"

Rebecca arched an eyebrow. "Really? Just look at her. She walks like a guy. She's got a guy's haircut. And that's men's cologne she wears."

"So?"

"So nothing. I'm just wondering."

"Just because a woman is gay doesn't mean she wants to be a man."

"I know that." Rebecca's expression turned into a wicked grin. "She's got a really nice ass, did you notice?"

Sarah couldn't help but laugh as they returned to the dining room table and their nearly-empty wine glasses. Sheepishly, she said, "Yes, I've noticed." Not a lie. She'd also noticed MJ's strong hands, the sinewy forearms, the thick shoulders good for holding onto… Sarah shook herself back to the conversation. "She's so nice too. Always pleasant. Always smiling. I like her."

"Me too. Can you imagine dating her? I wonder what that would be like."

"I think she'd be charming. You know? Like, she'd bring flowers and open doors. Pull out your chair. That kind of thing."

"I bet she's good in bed." Rebecca's voice dropped to a whisper. "They say lesbians are better lovers than men because they focus on their partner and not themselves."

"*They* say that? Who exactly is *they*?"

"I don't know." Rebecca laughed. "*They. Them.* The ones that know all that stuff."

This was Sarah's favorite pastime, the thing she loved most to do in the whole world. At least twice a week, sometimes more if their schedules permitted, Rebecca would come over and just spend time with her. They'd talk, they'd watch a movie, they'd take Jessie for a walk, they'd lie in lounge chairs in the back yard and just be together. Sarah had no idea if Rebecca was aware of how much these times meant to her. Frankly, she wasn't sure *she* understood why they meant so much. The only thing she was certain of was that she felt best, most relaxed, most like herself, when she was with Rebecca. And while she tried hard not to dwell on it, sometimes it couldn't be helped.

And dwelling on it scared the crap out of her.

"Well, I suppose I'd better get my butt home," Rebecca said eventually, stretching her arms over her head and groaning loudly.

Sarah averted her gaze and pretended to play with Jessie's sock. "Aw, do you have to?" she whined in a perfect imitation of her nine-year-old son.

Rebecca laughed and stood. "Believe me, I'd much rather stay here and drink wine with you." She gestured with her eyes at their empty glasses. "Unfortunately, dinner won't make itself." She playfully tugged Sarah's pony tail on her way into the living room.

"Somebody needs to invent that."

"What?"

"Dinner that makes itself."

Rebecca laughed as she gathered her bag and slipped into her shoes. "It would be revolutionary, that's for sure."

Sarah walked her to the door. "Thanks for keeping me company."

Rebecca nuzzled the dozing toddler still on Sarah's hip. "Bye-bye, Jessie. Be a good girl." She kissed the baby's head. "You need to put that child to bed." She placed a quick, chaste kiss on Sarah's lips and said, "Have fun at the teacher conference tonight. Bye." And she was off.

"Wave to Aunt Rebecca," Sarah said softly to her daughter, who could barely keep her eyes open as they stood on the stoop and watched their neighbor saunter down the street. Sarah tried not to look at Rebecca's ass, but it was a losing battle. It was always a losing battle. To Sarah, watching Rebecca was like watching living, breathing art. Her long limbs, her wavy brown hair, her graceful hands, her bow-shaped mouth, her warm hazel eyes…

Rebecca waved back at them once she reached her own front door, then went inside. Sarah sighed and followed suit, Jessie's now-sleeping form heavy in her arms. A glance at the clock told her she had roughly a half hour before the babysitter arrived to sit with Jessie while Sarah went to her teacher's conference. She made her way to the baby's room to deposit her in her crib. With Jeremy having dinner at his friend Eddie's house and Jessie down for the count, Sarah found herself with some unusual—and much desired—alone time.

Not wanting to waste one second, she headed straight for box number three of the packages MJ dropped off.

"Just some books" wasn't exactly the truth about the box's contents. There was a book, yes. There were also a few DVDs. She didn't like lying to Rebecca, but she just didn't think there was any way she'd understand. Or, she'd understand way too well. Sarah wasn't sure which would be worse.

Simply having the thin packages in her hand sent a thrilling shiver up her spine. *The Girl Sessions. Lesbian Love Volume 1. Afternoon Delight.* The book was *The Lesbian Sex Book.* Looking down at her new treasure trove, the thrill shifted immediately to guilt and then to fear. She glanced around, paranoid that somebody would see, that anybody walking by the house would feel the negative energy of her shame emanating right through the walls.

Inhale deeply.

Exhale slowly.

Sarah closed her eyes and talked herself back into calm. So what if somebody saw? She wasn't doing anything wrong. Was she? She was curious. She was exploring. So what? Whose business was it?

The fourth bedroom currently served as a home office—though if Skip had his way, it would harbor another baby in the near future—so Sarah grabbed the baby monitor and took her handful of contraband to the computer desk where she spread it out and just stared. The covers were racy. *Which makes sense since they're porn*, she thought, shaking her head at herself. Women of all shapes, sizes, and colors adorned the plastic cases in various states of undress. She had no idea where to start.

"What the hell am I doing?" she said quietly, though deep inside, she knew exactly what she was doing and why. She'd been struggling with—what? Curiosity? Unhappiness? Dissatisfaction? Feeling lost? Missing something? All of those clichés applied, and she'd tried for so long to compartmentalize, to put into a box the fact that she felt an overall restlessness in her life...tried to forget about it. She had so much. So, so much. Any woman would kill to have what she had: a handsome husband, beautiful children, a big house in an affluent section of the suburbs. She shopped when she wanted, bought what she wanted, went where she felt like going. To anybody looking in from the outside, her life was picture perfect.

But—and there was that cliché again—something *was* missing. Something she couldn't define. No, that wasn't quite true. Something she *didn't want* to define. The only time she felt whole, felt like herself, was when she was with Rebecca.

She couldn't pinpoint exactly when it started, but it scared the bejesus out of her. Still did, but not in the panicked, terrifying way it did in the beginning. It somehow settled in, simply became…fact. When she was with Rebecca, whether they were taking the kids someplace, at a social gathering, or alone in one of their houses like today, Sarah felt like she could breathe, like the world made sense, like she didn't need to question who she was or where she was in her life. Like everything was going to be okay.

She didn't examine it. She didn't roll it around. She simply accepted it. Which, if she was honest with herself, was the same as complete avoidance of the subject. Just accept it without discussion or thought or wonder. Simple acceptance was the easiest, least disturbing route.

Until about a month ago. She'd been watching a drama on television, one she watched weekly, despite the fact that it didn't always hold her interest. Skip snored on the couch next to her, the kids were in bed. Sarah alternated between the flat screen of the TV and the *Better Homes* magazine in her hand, flipping pages and then glimpsing up. Finishing an article on choosing the right color for your kitchen, she glanced up at the television just in time to see the very attractive Hispanic actress kiss the equally attractive blonde actress full on the mouth.

Sarah's own mouth went dry and it felt like her heart completely stopped. Not to mention the rush of wetness that hit her panties in a flash. In that moment, simultaneously, things became crystal clear, and Sarah felt like the stupidest woman on the planet. How could she not have seen it? How could she possibly not realize her now obvious attraction to women, to Rebecca? No wonder she counted the hours, the minutes, until they were in the same room together. Sarah was a smart woman, a college-educated, American female. How could she be such an idiot?

And what the hell was she going to do about it?

What *could* she do about it?

She'd looked over at her sleeping husband, his tousled sandy hair, the rough stubble on his face. He was a good man. He was a terrific father and a gentle, loving partner. They had a nice life together. The thought of disrupting all of it made her stomach roil, especially since she still didn't quite understand the implications.

Was she a lesbian? Was that possible?

Maybe she was bisexual. Could be. She liked that idea a little bit better. It seemed safer.

Maybe it was only Rebecca. Maybe she had some weird vibe that sang only to Sarah. That was possible, wasn't it? It was certainly the safest of all the choices. Yeah, she liked that one. It was only Rebecca. Somehow.

Sarah had picked up the remote and used the nifty rewind button the cable company so thoughtfully added to their features. Then she watched the kiss over again.

And over.

And over.

And over, sending surreptitious glances Skip's way to make sure he remained asleep.

Since that day, Sarah's every waking thought was filled with women. She looked at every female she encountered throughout the day and wondered about her. Did MJ think the way Sarah did? Was the cashier at the grocery store curious too? Could her yoga instructor feel Sarah looking at her neck, her mouth, her hands, her cleavage? Did Rebecca know? Did she ever think about the things Sarah thought of? Did she ever think of Sarah that way? If she did, she would have said something, wouldn't she? Unless, of course, she was as freaked out as Sarah. Then she'd be suffering in silence too. Just like Sarah. And suffering was exactly what she was doing.

Sarah roughly scrubbed a hand over her face. She could go around and around for hours, for days, like this. Hell, she *did*. It was no fun. With a groan borne of frustration, she slit the plastic wrap on *Afternoon Delight*. She decided to start there because, of the three covers, the women on this one were the most attractive to her. She popped the DVD into the computer, clicked the appropriate buttons, and waited for the action to begin.

It didn't take long, and Sarah thought her head might explode.

The acting was subpar and the plot was as bare bones as it could get, but the two leads were very attractive, very feminine, one blonde, one brunette, playing—of all things—*neighbors*.

"Jesus Christ. It figures," Sarah said aloud, quietly.

They were in a dining room and the blonde made a comment about how the baby was finally down for his nap. The brunette wasted no time making her move and six minutes into the film, they were kissing deeply. Fleetingly, Sarah thought they seemed much more genuine than the women on her TV show, less like two straight actresses kissing and much more like two lesbians who really wanted each other, who were very focused on one another, and who knew how to kiss a woman. By eleven minutes in, the blonde was naked and on her back on the dining room table, her shapely legs spread wide, her fingers buried in dark hair as the brunette drank from her center like she was dying of thirst.

"Oh, dear god…" Sarah whispered as she watched, a rush of heat flooding her entire body.

Almost as arousing as the sight of the two women were the sounds. The moans and groans, the whispered pleas and assurances, and the whimpers of pleasure did nothing but make Sarah painfully cognizant of the fact that she would need to change her underwear.

And when the blonde finally came, so did Sarah, only vaguely aware that she'd slipped her hand into her own shorts. She gripped the arm of the office chair until her knuckles went white, leg muscles twitching, gaze riveted to the screen.

There was more and Sarah would have stayed in her chair for hours had the doorbell not rung.

"Jesus Christ," she muttered, pulling her wet hand out of her shorts and attempting to button things up. She popped out the DVD, put it in its case, scooped up her treasures and ran into her bedroom. The his and hers closets pretty much ensured that Skip wouldn't accidentally find her stash, but just to be safe, she put it all in her sewing basket up on a shelf. The last time she'd sewed anything was when Jeremy was a baby. Nobody would think to look in there for anything valuable.

The doorbell rang again and Sarah swore.

A quick change from shorts to jeans, a stop in the bathroom to wash her hands, and Sarah was headed down the stairs just as the doorbell rang a third time and a voice from outside said with uncertainty, "Mrs. Holt?"

Sarah yanked the door open. "Hi, Kimmy. Sorry about that." She was out of breath and flushed, she was sure, but if her babysitter noticed, she said nothing. "Come on in."

Kimmy was her regular sitter and familiar with the house and the kids. She set her armload of books on the coffee table as Sarah gathered her purse and keys. "Jessie was tired today, so she's taking a little impromptu nap. Don't let her sleep past five, though. If she does, get her up or she won't sleep tonight."

"No prob." Kimmy plopped onto the couch and picked up a book. Glancing up at Sarah, she smiled and waved a dismissive hand. "Go. I've got it."

"You're the best. I shouldn't be long. Thanks."

The ride to the school was a blessing. Sarah used it to try to relax and calm her pounding heart and her racing blood, though getting the images from the DVD out of her head was not nearly as easy. Flashes of the beautiful blonde spread out on the dining room table like an invitation to a feast kept her mouth dry and her panties perpetually damp. She wasn't sure who turned her on more, the blonde offering herself so intimately to another woman or the brunette as the recipient of such a gift.

It was a definite toss-up.

At the school, she put the SUV in Park and took a deep breath. Giving her head a stern shaking, she hoped to rattle things back into place and get her mind focused. She nodded at people she knew as she entered the school and walked down the halls looking for Room 12. Hyperaware, her mind kept up a running commentary of every woman she passed. *Did this one have sex today? Oh, that one smells nice; I wonder what perfume she's wearing. I bet this one's breasts are beautiful. What does that one sound like when she has an orgasm?*

"Oh my god, stop it!" she whispered aloud as she approached her son's classroom. "Focus!" It was her first meeting with this teacher and the last thing she wanted was to come across as one of those parents who are clueless about her child's schooling. A deep cleansing breath, a check of her watch, and Sarah entered.

The woman behind the desk looked younger than she probably was. Short dark hair was tucked behind her ears and her gently made-up brown eyes seemed to take up more than their share of her face. Her skin was smooth as porcelain, her lashes and brows almost black, and her full lips shined with a recent coat of gloss. When she glanced at Sarah and smiled, the entire room felt warmer.

"Mrs. Holt?" She stood and held out her hand.

Sarah cleared her throat and reached for the hand, which was warm, soft, and Sarah held on a beat longer than she probably should have. "Sarah. Please."

"Hi, Sarah. I'm Cassidy Freeman. I'm so pleased to meet you. Jeremy is a great kid." She gestured to the chair next to her desk. "Have a seat."

Sarah thanked the gods above for the chair because she was certain her knees were about to give out. *Okay, so it's not just Rebecca,* she thought with a mixture of dismay and a little thrill. There was definitely something about Cassidy Freeman… Something… Sarah wet her lips, trying her damnedest to listen as Cassidy talked about Jeremy's strengths and weaknesses. Her eyes traveled from Cassidy's full lips across her jawline and down the side of her neck to the collarbone revealed by the open collar of her emerald green blouse. She stopped at what she knew from the movie *The English Patient* was called the super sternum notch, that delicate spot at the base of a woman's throat. Right then, Sarah wanted nothing more than to run her tongue over that skin.

"So, other than that whole talking thing, he's doing great," Cassidy was saying. Sarah glanced up to meet her eyes, which held concern. "Sarah? Are you all right?"

Sarah blinked several times and forced a smile onto her face. "I'm good." She hoped her nodding and feigned enthusiasm weren't over the top. "No, I'm good," she repeated, only one clear thought in her head.

What the hell am I going to do?

THE TEACHER

Jeremy Holt's mother—who was totally hot, despite seeming a little dazed—was Cassidy Freeman's last appointment for the evening. Thank god because she was so excited about her date that night, she felt as if she'd spent the day constantly squirming in her chair like some of her students. Parent-teacher conferences probably ended up being a lifesaver, no matter how much she'd muttered and resented them all day. If she'd gone home on time, Cassidy knew she would have driven herself to the brink of insanity pacing her apartment and trying to decide what to wear. This way, it was after five o'clock. She was meeting Deb at the restaurant at 7:30, so she had barely two hours to shower, change, and get there. Cassidy worked much better under pressure.

An uneventful drive home, a quick zip through the mail, a quick feeding of the cat, and Cassidy was in the shower reflecting on what little she knew about Deb Crawford.

In her mid-thirties, Deb was the president of her own payroll company. She was fairly well-known locally, her company growing by leaps and bounds and participating in many local charity events. So... confident and financially well-off. Those were definite plusses to Cassidy. She'd spent three years supporting her last girlfriend—both monetarily and psychologically—and it was more than exhausting. She was not in any hurry to deal with that again. According to Cassidy's friend who was setting them up, Deb had been in a relationship for ten years, but had been single for almost two years since then. She had a bit of a reputation for womanizing, and that gave Cassidy the slightest bit of trepidation, but she was willing to find out for herself. Besides, she was a little bit fascinated by Deb's success and drive. She was looking forward to exploring those subjects. Strong, intelligent women were such a turn-on.

Over the past few days, Cassidy gave great thought to her outfit, weighing the pros and cons of different choices and what they'd say about her. Too sexy could give Deb the impression Cassidy was expecting something more would happen than dinner. Too casual could mean either she didn't really care or she had no fashion sense, neither of which was true. So, she wracked her brains to come up with something suitably in between. The resulting black slacks, black camisole, and ivory silk blouse was pretty damn perfect, if she did say so herself. Simple, classy, feminine, yet confident.

"What do you think?" she asked Hermione as she studied herself in the full-length mirror. The cat meowed.

"You're right. I almost forgot the jewelry." She kept it all subtle, not wanting to overdo it. The necklace was a muted turquoise oval on a black thong that gave a warm splash of color to the outfit. Simple diamond studs went in her ears and she tucked her dark hair behind them. An understated touch of makeup, a spritz of her Coco perfume, and she was ready.

Hermione yawned when Cassidy kissed the top of her head and grabbed a jacket. "No parties while I'm gone. Leave a light on for me, okay?"

Being a weeknight, the restaurant wasn't terribly busy, but had enough of a crowd to keep the wait staff moving at a steady pace. Cassidy arrived at 7:25 and before Deb, so she grabbed a seat at the bar and ordered herself a glass of the house Cabernet, sipping as she took in her surroundings. She remembered when it was a lesbian bar several years ago. As was the case any time somebody tried to open one in this city, it didn't last long. But instead of changing endless hands and renaming what was essentially the same bar over and over again, this time, it was purchased by two lesbian business partners who made it into a nice, upscale restaurant—that happened to have a bar. There was no dance floor, only a corner piano where various jazz musicians played during happy hours and beyond, loudly enough to enjoy, but not so loud as to make conversation difficult. The menu was simple and elegant, the wine list extensive, and the atmosphere one of warmth and contentment. Cassidy loved it here.

At 7:45, she pulled her phone from her clutch and set it in view on the bar, in case Deb tried to get ahold of her for some reason. She debated a second glass of wine, but the bartender interrupted her.

"Waiting for somebody?" he asked. He had that lean, slightly effeminate look of a guy who played on Cassidy's team. His sandy hair was very short, and his eyes were an interesting light brown, warm and kind.

"Sort of a blind date," Cassidy replied. "I know what she looks like, but we've never met."

"Internet date?"

Cassidy shook her head. "God, no," she laughed, then gave a mock shudder. "Set up by a friend of a friend."

"Ah. Well, my name is Jason, and I say relax and have another glass of wine."

"I say you're right, Jason. I'm Cassidy." They shook hands as they chuckled together, and he poured her some more wine.

By the time another twenty minutes went by, Cassidy was feeling a mix of hurt, anger, and embarrassment. It was one thing to sit at a bar alone for a few minutes while waiting for your date to arrive. It was quite another to sit at the bar alone for nearly an hour. Should she call Deb? Did she screw up the day/time/place? She slid her finger across the touchscreen of her phone to activate it, and checked to make sure she hadn't missed a call or text. Nothing.

She sent a quick text to her friend Amy, who'd initially suggested the date, asking if she'd heard anything from Deb. Then she waited.

The restaurant crowd increased a bit and there was a steady din of conversation all around her. Several people took up residence along the bar, keeping Jason busy. He glanced Cassidy's way as he served a customer, gave her a wink. She watched him work, amazed as she always was by the efficiency of most bartenders. He wrote nothing down, mixed drinks in no time flat, smiled and laughed, flirted with men and women alike, and kept the whole area clean and wiped down. She wondered absently if he made a decent living, thought he probably went home with a nice pile of tips.

On the bar, her phone vibrated and she opened the text from Amy. It said simply, "She there yet? I haven't heard anything."

"Oh, you have got to be kidding," Cassidy muttered, her lips pressed together in a straight, thin line. Was this really happening? Was she really being stood up? Didn't that only happen in movies and romance novels? Who did that in real life? Then a worse thought occurred to her: What if Deb had peeked in, seen her, then turned around and fled? Cassidy knew she was an attractive woman, but this uncertainty was messing with her head, and she felt her self-esteem circling the drain.

"Nothing yet?" Jason's voice yanked her out of her wallowing, and she looked up to meet his gentle eyes.

"Nope." She sighed, trying to hide her embarrassment.

"Seriously? No text or voicemail or anything? Who does that?"

Cassidy loved his indignation on her behalf and felt a sudden urge to hug him. "I know, right?"

"Well, screw her. Him?" He cocked an eyebrow at her and she smiled.

"Her."

"Well, screw her. It's her loss." He topped off her glass.

"You're damn right it is," she said with a nod, hoping she sounded tougher and more determined than she felt.

Jason hustled down the bar to take care of a customer. Cassidy unlocked her phone and opened it to her Facebook page, trying not to dwell on the anger, hurt, and embarrassment that was beginning to blanket her like a fog. She couldn't help herself; she went to Deb's page, but there was nothing incriminating there. She'd learned by watching her students that most people were rarely careful about the information they posted and who might see it. Deb's status hadn't been updated since yesterday, so there was nothing saying she was at some club or out to dinner with friends or avoiding the date she was supposed to be on right now. Cassidy wasn't sure if she was happy or sad about the lack of material; it would be nice to know one way or another. Wouldn't it?

A thought came to her and her thumbs were moving over her keyboard before she could stop herself. She updated her status.

How long can a beautiful woman sit alone at a bar before somebody offers to buy her a drink?

She reread it, smiled, and hit Post. At least Amy would see it. And if Amy saw it, Deb would eventually hear about it. Passive-aggressive? *Oh, yes,* Cassidy thought. *My mother taught me well. And I'm totally okay with it.*

She set down her phone and picked up her wine just as Jason approached her with a small plate and set it in front of her along with a rolled napkin containing silverware.

"Just a little something to help the wine sit okay," he said. "On the house."

Touched, Cassidy didn't know what to say.

"I repeat—screw her. She obviously doesn't know what she's missing." He went off to tend to his clientele.

"If I was a guy," Cassidy said under her breath, "I'd totally ask *you* out."

The plate before her had a small variety of appetizers...some bruschetta, raw veggies and a generous dollop of what looked like homemade hummus, and a ramekin of warm artichoke dip. It was only in that moment that she realized how hungry she was and dug in, trying hard not to think about the sympathy she always felt for people she saw eating alone in a restaurant. How many of them had been stood up?

The food was outstanding and Cassidy wondered if she was making any humming noises as she ate; it was that good. The hummus was smooth and flavorful, the garlic there but not overpowering. The bruschetta was tangy and delicious and the artichoke dip was so warm and creamy, she considered abandoning the crackers and simply eating it with a spoon. For twenty minutes, she actually thought about nothing but the food and the wine and let herself just enjoy it. She was dabbing at the corners of her mouth with the linen napkin when a voice next to her posed a question.

"What did you think?"

Cassidy turned to meet warm hazel eyes that studied her through rimless glasses. A woman in a white chef's coat stood next to her, a delicate smile on her face. She was about the same height standing as Cassidy was sitting on the tall barstool, and she leaned one elbow on the bar as she cocked her head. Her hair was cut in a simple bob, highlighted with toasty chestnut and subtle streaks of gold. Cassidy put her in her early to mid-fifties and there was something about her...something that drew Cassidy, that almost called to her. It was a feeling that both comforted and discomfited her. She cleared her throat.

"Well, as you can see," she said, waving a hand at her very nearly empty plate, "it was awful. Horrendous, really. The chef should be ashamed."

The woman nodded, feigning a grave expression. "I'm so sorry for your dissatisfaction. Though it does seem that you ate all of it."

"Of course I ate all of it. I had to be absolutely sure of its awfulness, didn't I?"

"I see. Well, the chef happens to be me and an unhappy customer is very bad for business. I hope you'll allow me to make it up to you."

Never one for such open, obvious flirtation, Cassidy was surprised to realize how much she was enjoying this little game and she loved that this intriguing woman was playing along. She propped her chin in her hand and her elbow on the bar. "An interesting offer. What exactly did you have in mind?"

"I thought maybe I could recover my reputation by making you brunch on Sunday morning."

"Brunch?"

"Yes. Right here."

Cassidy narrowed her eyes in playful suspicion. "This restaurant isn't open for brunch."

"That's true."

"Do you own it?"

"I do."

God, what was it about her? Cassidy had never felt such a pull before, but somehow, it didn't frighten her. She knew without a doubt that she could very well go home with this woman right now without thinking twice and that realization didn't freak her out at all.

"You want to make brunch for me on Sunday? Here? Just you and me?"

"I do." The chef was completely relaxed, which Cassidy would normally find cocky. Normally, she'd wonder what kind of reputation this woman had, assume she was probably some kind of womanizer. But again, there was something…different. And Cassidy wanted to be around her.

"I have one request."

The chef arched an eyebrow, waiting.

"Your name?"

The delicate smile widened, and dimples appeared. Cassidy nearly swooned. "Kate Martindale. Pleased to meet you." She held out her hand.

"Cassidy Freeman. A pleasure." Kate's hand was warm and strong and Cassidy had a sudden feeling of safety, of contentment, of comfort. She almost didn't let go.

"I should get back to the kitchen," Kate said, her eyes never leaving Cassidy's and their hands still linked. "Can't afford any more dissatisfied customers."

"Absolutely not," Cassidy agreed. "I don't want to show up for brunch and find a dozen other people." She caught her bottom lip between her teeth to keep from smiling.

"Oh, no. That will not be the case, I assure you. Just come to the front door on Sunday at eleven and I'll be waiting for you. Yes?"

"I look forward to it."

"Me too."

They stayed for a few moments more until Kate finally let Cassidy's hand slide out of her grasp. With a small wave, she headed back through the swinging door to the kitchen.

Cassidy let out her breath. "Oh, wow." She felt a giggle bubbling up from her chest and worked hard to keep it tamped down; this was not the place to act like a schoolgirl. Instead, she gestured to Jason for her tab.

He brought it to her. As she signed, he leaned forward on his forearms and said, "Hope your night wasn't a total bust."

She lifted her gaze to his, noted his mischievous grin. "Nope. In fact, it turned out better than I expected." Stretching toward him, she kissed his cheek. "Thank you."

He flushed a light pink and took his leave.

Cassidy picked up her stuff and headed out into the night. As she breathed in the crisp autumn air, she said aloud, "Deb? Deb who?"

"I cannot *believe* I just did that. Oh, my god."

Kate Martindale walked back into the kitchen of her restaurant in somewhat of a daze, feeling both energized and horrified by what had taken place at the bar just minutes ago. She'd asked a woman out. A woman she'd never met. A woman about whom she knew squat. A woman whose very presence in her restaurant caused Kate to feel warm and soft inside. It was the weirdest thing she'd ever experienced. Jason had come in and told her about this hot chick at the bar who had been stood up by her blind date. Her female blind date. Kate had peeked out at her and felt an instant, inexplicable stab of desire to know her better.

"Did what?" Jason asked as he breezed in to fill his five-gallon pail with ice from the icemaker. One glance at Kate and his eyes went wide. "Holy shit, you asked her out, didn't you? *That's* what she meant!" He set the bucket down, wrapped his arms around Kate, and twirled her in a circle. "I'm so proud of you!"

"Oh, for god's sake. Put me down." Kate smacked his shoulder. "And what do you mean, 'that's what she meant?'"

"She said her night had turned out better than she'd expected. I wasn't sure what she meant, but now I know."

Kate blinked at him.

"This is good, Katie. This is very good."

"What's good?" Charlotte Becker, Kate's sous chef, asked as she reached into the refrigerator.

"Kate asked her out." Jason's face beamed like a proud father.

"The hottie at the bar?" Charlotte mimicked Jason's earlier wide-eyed expression. "Oh, my god. Did she say yes?"

"She did." Kate still felt a little dazed. "I'm making her brunch on Sunday."

"Ooo, brunch. Very good call." Jason nodded his approval. "Not as intimate as dinner, but not as casual as coffee. Nicely done."

Kate looked at him, her eyes beseeching. "What the hell was I thinking, Jay?"

Jason tilted his head in a gesture of fondness and sympathy and reached out to touch her cheek. "Oh, Katie, you deserve this. You deserve to be happy. Who knows if this will go anywhere? It's way too soon to know that. But maybe you'll have some fun for a few hours. There's nothing wrong with that, and it's nothing for you to feel guilty about. Okay?"

Kate nodded. "Okay."

She hoped she sounded more confident than she felt.

She hoped she wasn't a disappointment to Cassidy Freeman.

***

"Cassidy Freeman. Cassidy Freeman." Kate rolled the name around on her tongue as she pulled into her driveway. "What a great name." Saying it aloud conjured up the oval face of creamy skin, the enormous brown eyes, and the short hair the color and richness of dark melted chocolate. "And let's not pretend you didn't notice the rest of the package," she muttered to herself, distinctly remembering how hard it was to keep her eyes on Cassidy's face and not travel over her breasts, her hips, her thighs. God, she was pretty.

And young.

Kate didn't really notice until she approached her. Cassidy couldn't be older than thirty-five, almost twenty years younger than Kate. She almost chickened out right then, but Cassidy didn't seem to be the least bit put off. Kate liked to think she looked a bit younger than she was, but she didn't look forty. Cassidy not only accepted Kate's flirtatious comments, but she flirted back. That had to be a good sign, didn't it?

She unlocked the side door and dropped her stuff on the small, round kitchen table, then wandered into the living room.

"Hi, Cammie," she said to the heavyset, African-American woman sitting in the La-Z-y Boy and knitting.

"Hello there, Kate. How was your night?"

Kate crossed to the hospital bed and kissed her brother on his pale, cool forehead. "Hi, Handsome."

Keith didn't acknowledge her. He didn't blink. His watery blue eyes stared straight up, and Kate was never sure if he saw the swirls in the ceiling or something in his own mind; sometimes his gaze was incredibly intense and others, it was just vague.

"My night was pretty good," Kate said honestly. "How about his?"

"Calm." Cammie stood and packed up her yarn and needles. "He had a little bit of Gatorade and kept it down. I gave him a sponge bath and washed his hair, so he smells better."

"Oh, good. He needed that."

"He's due for his next dose in about a half hour." Cammie hefted her tote bag over her shoulder.

"Got it." Kate pulled a wheeled stool across the hardwood floor and sat next to the bed.

"Mike will be here tomorrow at eleven," Cammie told her. "I'll take over at six."

"Perfect. Thanks, Cammie."

"You have a good night, honey."

The door clicked shut as Kate set her chin on her forearms on top of the metal bed rail. She tried hard not compare this Keith—

withered, painfully thin, helpless—with the strong, capable man her little brother had grown into over the years. He was only forty-seven, but he looked decades older. His hair—what was left of it—had gone almost completely gray and looked flat and lifeless most of the time. His cheeks were sunken into his face, his skin had a gray pallor, and all his muscle tone had melted away until he was six feet three inches of nothing but skin and bones. She reached out to touch his stubbly face.

"I met a girl tonight, K-Two," she said to him, using the childhood nickname she'd given him when he was ten. "You'd have been proud of me. I went right up to her and asked her if I could make her brunch. Can you believe that? That's something you would've done. Not me." She wasn't certain, but she thought she saw the corner of Keith's mouth quirk up just a little. "She's so pretty. And a lot younger than me, I think. I'm kind of nervous about that, but there was just something about her. I couldn't resist. I made her up an appetizer plate and sent it to her on the house. Can you believe *that?*" If she closed her eyes, she could almost hear Keith chuckling, teasing, *What? You actually* gave *something away? For free?* He loved to mock her serious business side, the side that kept track of every extra drink, every order of steak fries that was larger than it should have been, every loaf of Italian bread that got tossed at the end of the night. He called her Scrooge. With great love and affection, of course.

She told him she'd be right back, then went to the kitchen to make herself a cup of decaf. When it was ready, she returned to the living room to find her little brother trying to sit up. Kate set down her mug and went to him.

"Hey, what's going on, buddy?" she asked, hating that she now talked to him like he was a child.

"Gotta go," he told her, his voice raspy from lack of use, but matter-of-fact in tone.

"Oh, okay. Where are we going?" In the three weeks he'd been here, she'd learned to stay calm, to go with his delusions and hallucinations rather than try to correct him. It wasn't always easy; she missed him so.

"Gotta pick up firewood." Keith tugged his blanket so it was around his shoulders. "Jack and Ricky are meeting me."

"Oh, yeah. I remember you telling me that." Kate helped wrap the blanket around him. "Let's make sure we put your jacket on, though. It's chilly."

"Okay."

Kate made the pretense of bundling him up. After a minute, he turned to look at her, blinked once, and asked, "You coming?"

She only hesitated for a second. "Absolutely," she replied, and climbed into the bed next to him. It was a tight fit, but they worked and shifted until they were both comfortable, her with her arm around him just like when they were little kids and Keith had a bad dream. He'd climb into her twin bed with her, certain that she'd protect him. The memory made her eyes well up. He sighed contentedly and rested his head on her shoulder.

"Comfy?" she asked.

He nodded, then said quietly, "Thank you."

It was amazing how quickly he could go from delusional to perfectly coherent. It was also amazing how two one-syllable words could put such a lump in her throat. "No thanks necessary, little brother. No thanks necessary."

As she tightened her hold on him and felt him drifting off to sleep, she thought about one of the regulars at the restaurant, an older woman in her seventies, very nice, and very religious. When she learned about Keith's diagnosis, she said to Kate, "Well, it's God's will. He's calling your brother home. It's a wonderful honor to be summoned by Him." Kate had been able to bite her tongue and simply nod at the woman, but inside, she was seething. Now, as she held the shell of what once was a strapping, athletic man, she felt that old familiar anger bubbling up like lava.

A wonderful honor? Really? I beg to differ. Look at him. He's been whittled down to nothing. He can't eat. He's in constant pain. He's on so many drugs, he's like a junkie. He needs his big sister to help him take a crap and to wipe his ass. Where's this honor you talk about? What is the point of so much suffering? What did my brother ever do to deserve this fate? God can go fuck himself as far as I'm concerned.

Keith whimpered in his fitful sleep and Kate pulled him closer. She kissed his head, which smelled like the baby shampoo Cammie must have used on him earlier. "It's okay, K-Two. I've got you. Don't you worry. Nothing's going to get you. I'm right here and I've got you."

***

A couple gentle knocks on the side door jerked Kate awake to late morning sunlight streaming through the windows of the living room. She stretched, her back protesting the hour she'd spent in Keith's bed. Unfortunately, the living room couch wasn't a whole lot more comfortable; at this point, it's where she slept most often, not wanting to be far in case Keith needed something during the night. Plus, he was now getting his morphine every two-to-three hours as needed.

She tried not to think about what that meant.

"Morning, Kate."

Mike was not at all what Kate expected in a Hospice worker when she first met him. First of all, he was huge. Not fat, just huge, probably six four, with shoulders almost the width of Kate's arm span. He was completely bald, with large gages in his earlobes and—according to him—seventeen tattoos, all covered by his clothing, as required by his employer.

"God, is it eleven already?"

"Almost. Rough night?" He walked to Keith's bed and rubbed an enormous hand over her brother's head. "Hey, buddy. How're you doing today?"

The dichotomy of his imposing size and his gentle demeanor always surprised Kate. She was reminded daily by Mike that looks can be deceiving.

"I crawled in bed with him for a little while, and my body is now reminding me that I'm not twenty-five."

Mike chuckled. "I'll put some coffee on. You look like you could use it."

It took a very special kind of human to do what Mike and Cammie and all the wonderful people she'd met along this journey of Keith's did. They didn't show pity or over-sympathize. They were simply gentle and nurturing and compassionate. Their touches, their voices, their expressions, everything radiated kindness and warmth. Kate would never understand how they could be around so much sadness, sickness, and death all the time and not want to just crawl into a hole. Or scream. Or break things. Whatever the answer, she would be forever grateful to them. At least Keith would pass away with some modicum of dignity thanks to the humanity of the caretakers surrounding him.

***

After two mugs of Mike's excellent coffee and a quick shower, Kate kissed her brother on the forehead, stroked a hand over his now clean-shaven cheek, and worked hard to tamp down the sudden feeling that she didn't have a lot of time left with him. Honestly, it would be a relief to not have to care for him on such an intense level—it was emotionally and physically draining, and she felt like a limp dishrag so much of the time. But the thought of life without her little brother put a lump so solidly in her throat that it felt permanent. Standing next to his bed for a few extra moments allowed her to collect herself and blink back the sudden tears that threatened. She took a deep breath and thanked Mike, then headed out.

The restaurant was open for lunch and Charlotte usually had no trouble handling things, but Kate liked to wander in and sit in the office. She looked at potential new dishes for specials, updated the website, talked to suppliers. Sometimes, she just read the paper. It was her second home, and lately, it was her escape, her sanctuary. On her way, she made her usual stop at her favorite local coffee shop and was greeted with a huge smile by the same young girl who worked there every day.

"Morning, Lindsay," she said as the girl flashed her that cute smile. She couldn't have been more than twenty or twenty-five, but Kate thought she was adorable, often joking with Jason that she felt like a dirty old man whenever she ordered there. That was funny because Lindsay was *so* not her type, regardless of age. She had a funky, angular haircut dyed jet-black, a hoop in her nose, another in her eyebrow, and a tattoo on the back of her neck. But there was something about her energy, her smile, and positive attitude. Kate never once saw her without that smile; customers loved her. Kate absently wondered if Lindsay'd be interested in waitressing for her. She'd make more money, Kate was sure about that.

"Good almost afternoon," Lindsay said. "The usual?"

"Yes, please. As large as I can get."

"You got it." She took Kate's money and turned to the counter.

As Lindsay went to work on Kate's drink, Kate gazed out the window at the passing traffic. The sun was shining; it was turning into a beautiful fall day, and she wished she could show Keith, maybe play hooky for the afternoon and make him go on a hike with her. It was a little game they played before he got sick; she'd ask him to go with her and he'd whine and complain the whole time, while simultaneously picking up cool rocks and pointing out different species of trees or birds. He loved nature. He just didn't want to admit it.

The lump returned and Kate tried to shake her head of the sad thoughts that seemed determined to fog over her today. Her mind suddenly handed her a picture of Cassidy Freeman.

Oh, that's much better, she thought, not bothering to hide her grin as Lindsay called out her coffee.

"Well, I'm glad my coffee makes you so happy," she said with a wink at Kate.

"Oh, it does," Kate told her, meaning it. "Thank you."

She left the coffee shop with a much springier step than she had when she arrived and the sun seemed a little bit brighter as she drove to the restaurant.

It was time to plan a brunch menu.

THE BARISTA

Lindsay Curtis knew two things really well: coffee and people. It was her knowledge of people that kept her mind occupied throughout the day as she served them the best coffee in the city. After all, being a barista wasn't exactly brain surgery. But she loved the different personalities that she got to observe as they came and left the shop, especially her regulars. Those were the people who interested her most.

Like the chef. Lindsay didn't know her name and only knew she was a chef because she'd come into the shop more than once in her white chef's coat. She never arrived earlier than ten a.m., she always ordered the same thing—a double latte with a shot of espresso—and she always looked just a little bit sad. There was something very attractive about her, and that made Lindsay chuckle because the chef was probably older than her mother, but she was very striking. She had great skin, a simple but classy haircut, and kind eyes that peered out from behind her rimless glasses. She was little—maybe five-three —but her presence seemed bigger, and when she smiled, like today, her entire face lit up. Lindsay found her intriguing.

The oversized, coffee-mug clock on the wall above the door told her she had one more hour of work. Today was Lindsay's favorite day of the week. She got off a little earlier than other days and her girlfriend, Cara, had a late meeting and wouldn't be home until seven. That left Lindsay nearly four full hours in Cara's apartment for her favorite pastime: writing erotica.

A tall, reed-thin man ordered a cappuccino and Lindsay went to work on it, her mind wandering as she did so.

She fit the bill pretty well as far as looking like a writer of lesbian erotica, or so she thought. She had an edgy appearance. Her mother hated the severity of her haircut—short, all sharply cut angles—but Lindsay loved it, felt it fit her perfectly. She was, however, tiring of the jet black and was toying with what color should be next. Electric blue was high on the list. She thought she'd been pretty tame with the piercings—though the one in her eyebrow almost sent her father to the R wing of the local hospital. She had a few more in mind for her ears, but she was going to let things die down a bit before she shook them up again; her parents weren't getting any younger. Most of the time, though, she was proud of the fact that she *looked* like what she *was*. And by "what she was," she meant, "what she wanted to be." Writing erotica wasn't a simple pastime for her; she wanted to make a career of it. Hey, the chick who wrote *Fifty Shades of Grey* did it. Why couldn't she?

Early afternoon was generally a slow time at the shop. The lunch rush was over and the early evening rush hadn't begun. Lindsay busied herself for her last half hour wiping down tables and stacking clean mugs.

She was young to be writing what she wrote, and she knew it. At twenty-three, she hardly had scads of experience to shape her erotic stories from. What she did have was a love of reading, a large collection of lesbian movies—including an impressive array of porn—and one hell of an imagination. The combination of the three worked wonders for her as far as ideas went. She had no clue where her love of erotica came from; her parents certainly weren't free spirits or raging liberals or anything of the sort. They were still pretending she hadn't told them she was gay. They'd come around, she was sure. They always did; it just took them a while. In the meantime, she was going to keep her writing a secret from them. If they couldn't handle a tiny hole in her eyebrow, there was no way they'd be able to accept that she wrote stories containing words like *pussy* and *nipple* and *orgasm*. Her mother would simply keel over.

Frankie Moore.

She smiled as she said the name aloud softly while she packed up her things and got ready for the walk to Cara's. It was a good name for an erotica writer and she'd thought long and hard before settling on it. Frankie was masculine and feminine at the same time, ensuring she'd appeal to both the butches and the femmes and every lesbian in between...and maybe some straight women too. Moore was, of course, a play on words—she hoped after reading one of her stories, a reader would want more.

The chef had given her something to think about, namely a story with older characters in it. Unlike many of her peers, Lindsay was mature enough to see that the world did not revolve simply around her generation. Hello, there *are* lesbians who are middle aged and older; they have sex too. Don't they deserve their own stories? It seemed to her that the overwhelming majority of erotica she'd read included characters ranging from early twenties to mid-thirties. Oh, sure, there was an occasional one with an older character, but they were few and far between. Many of the e-mails she received in response to some of her work had pointed out this very discrepancy and asked if she could remedy the situation.

The chef could certainly help her do that. She just had to figure out the right scenario for her...

Lindsay used soy milk and made herself a tall Chai latte with extra spice, then put it in a to-go cup, donned her jacket, and swung her backpack over her shoulder.

"See you tomorrow, Linz," Chet said to her as she headed for the door. He was the owner, had been for nearly ten years, and Lindsay adored his kind heart and easygoing manner.

"Bright and early," she replied with a wave.

The breeze was a little chilly, but the sun was shining sporadically and Lindsay had plenty to occupy her mind as she made the trek to Cara's tiny apartment. She loved the city, loved being close enough to walk just about anywhere. She didn't officially live with Cara—they'd only been together for a few months and frankly, Cara's apartment was too small for two of them—but she hoped that at some point down the road, she'd have a place nearby that she could actually call home. Would that place be with Cara? It was possible. She certainly hoped so. Cara hadn't given her a key yet, but Lindsay knew where the spare was hidden and Cara didn't mind that she used it. Lindsay was pretty sure her own key would be coming soon.

They'd met at a party where they each had mutual friends. Lindsay could still remember the exact moment when she laid eyes on Cara, her chestnut hair loose around her shoulders, her startling green eyes catching Lindsay's and holding them. She'd gotten a friend to introduce her. Cara was older than Lindsay, worked as a massage therapist, and her aura of confidence was nearly visible—a complete and utter turn-on for Lindsay. A couple of beers, a tequila shot or two, and they'd ended up making out in the bathroom.

Cara was a fabulous kisser, her mouth soft and warm, the kiss equal parts giving and taking. Lindsay had simply floated away.

The smile that came to her lips couldn't be helped as she walked along and reminisced. Lindsay had had other relationships—though, admittedly, not many—but her love for Cara was different, ran deeper, was much more...mature. Lindsay actually felt as if she'd grown up while she dated Cara. If that was because of their nearly fifteen-year age difference, she wasn't certain.

"Ha," she said aloud to nobody. "Look at me, thinking like an adult. What would my parents say?"

Cara's one-bedroom apartment was one fraction of an enormous house on a tree-lined street of enormous houses. At some point in time, it was broken up into six separate units, and Lindsay often wondered what it must have looked like a hundred years ago when it was a one-family home. The lobby was certainly once part of the grand foyer. Its huge staircase, elegant in its simplicity, demanded the eye as you walked in. The owner and landlord lived in the ground floor apartment to Lindsay's right. He was a stickler about some of his rules, but he kept the place in tip-top shape. The wood banister gleamed in the gentle light of the opulent chandelier that hung from the high ceiling. The burgundy carpet runner on the stairs had been recently vacuumed, and the leaded glass windows sparkled in the afternoon's sunlight.

On the second floor, Lindsay stopped in front of Cara's door and felt up along the molding, a painfully obvious place to keep the spare key. She opened the door, returned the key, and went inside, breathing in the lingering scent of Cara's perfume. The apartment was small, but brightly sunny, with gleaming hardwood floors and large windows. Lindsay once inquired why Cara didn't have a house and she replied simply that she loved her little apartment, so why make a change? Directly in front of the door along the wall on the left was a kitchenette that was open to the living room, a roomy enough space with windows on two sides. Cara didn't have a lot of furniture, but what she did have was of decent quality. She liked to save her money and buy the best rather than buy cheaply to get more. The couch was soft burgundy leather and there was a matching oversized chair and ottoman. Small oak end tables, a matching coffee table, and an oval area rug in earth tones brought the room together—modest in size but elegant in design. Cara had a great eye for color and layout.

Lindsay was always telling her she could fall back on interior design if massage therapy didn't work out for her.

The bedroom was generous for such a small place. Cara was able to fit her queen-sized bed, a dresser, and a small desk without it feeling too cramped. Lindsay dropped her bag on the bed, shucked off her jacket, and booted up the laptop that seemed to be waiting for her on the uncluttered surface of the desk.

Not the most comfortable of desk chairs, it would do, and Lindsay sat down, facing the window. It was the only request she made; she needed to be able to gaze outside while she was writing. Admittedly, her craft consisted of a lot of staring off into space, and she preferred to stare at nature rather than an empty wall. Cara even mounted a small birdfeeder outside the window so Lindsay might have some entertainment on days when she found herself stuck for ideas.

Word opened quickly and Lindsay scanned through the last few paragraphs of the story she was currently working on. It was for a collection of "first time" stories she'd been asked to contribute to, and it was shaping up to be quite sexy, if she did say so herself. But when she tried to insert her mind back into the action, she had trouble—her thoughts kept drifting to the chef and what kind of character she might make. So, rather than type, Lindsay gazed out the window and outlined what kind of a personality she'd give the chef.

In her genre of writing, Lindsay's criteria were a bit different than the average writer. She did not subscribe to the common PWP (Plot? What plot?) form of erotica writing. She preferred to give her characters at least some depth and personality before she allowed them to have sex. While she couldn't get *too* detailed—a surefire way to lose an erotica reader—she did like to make them seem at least somewhat realistic. Most erotica readers want to insert themselves into the story; that's why they read. Lindsay wanted to make sure her readers could relate, at least a little, to the characters she created. It was important to her. Anybody could write a sex scene. It took talent to make it feel real.

The chef had an air of authority about her, a confidence that bred attraction. She was a small woman, but she walked tall, seemed larger than she was just because of her aura of certainty. So Lindsay decided she would own her own restaurant.

"Now," Lindsay said aloud. "Is she a player?" She thought about how many beautiful women might come into a nice restaurant on any given evening. A wicked grin spread out on her face as she realized it could be, probably would be, dozens. "Hell of a smorgasbord," she commented, recognizing that in addition to customers, there would be waitresses, a hostess, maybe a female bartender, and a couple of other cooks. So many to choose from. "Player, it is."

She opened a new document and began to type.

Lindsay was surprised at how quickly the story came to her. And it was *hot*. The chef wasn't just a player; she was insatiable. She began her evening by having her way with the leggy hostess in her office before business hours. The desk served as the perfect surface and the hostess's black skirt made for easy access. Later in the evening, she cornered her bartender in the basement and fucked her roughly on a case of Captain Morgan. As her clientele began to trickle out the door and the hour slid toward closing time, the chef eyed two pretty young things at the bar and seriously wondered if she could charm her way into a ménage a trios.

By the time Lindsay pulled her attention from her computer screen and returned to her own world, the sun was just about gone and the bedroom dimmed in the dusk. She blinked several times and rubbed at her scratchy eyes. She noticed the dampness in her panties at the exact same time she heard Cara's key in the lock.

"Oh, baby, timing is everything," she whispered.

In every way that Lindsay was edgy, Cara was not. With a sprinkle of freckles across her nose and a gentle smile on her face, she looked more like the girl next door than the partner of a lesbian sex writer, and she came through the front door with no clue as to Lindsay's state of mind.

"Linz?" she called as she tossed her keys on the table inside the door and flipped through the small stack of mail.

"Right here," Lindsay replied, knowing her proximity startled Cara, but Lindsay's mouth was on hers before she could utter more than a surprised gasp.

Envelopes and fliers fluttered to the floor as Cara gave in to the kiss. It was always like this, always a…melting during their first kiss before lovemaking. Cara was older, but Lindsay preferred to "drive," as she liked to call it, and took the wheel every chance she could. Cara didn't seem to mind.

Two steps and Cara gave a small grunt as her back hit the door. Lindsay kissed across her chin and down her neck, talking as she went. "You look good enough to eat, baby," she said, her voice throaty.

"Yeah?" Cara breathed, hands in Lindsay's hair.

"Yeah. And that's exactly what I plan on doing." In one quick movement, she pulled Cara's shirt up and over her head, tossed it to the hardwood, and cupped Cara's small breasts through the purple lace bra Lindsay'd given her for her birthday.

"Been writing, have we?" Cara's chuckle turned to a groan as precise fingers closed on her nipples.

"Yup. Lucky you."

They made their way slowly to the small bedroom, dropping articles of clothing as they went. Lindsay's shirt, Cara's pants, Cara's bra, Lindsay's socks. This kamikaze lovemaking used to bother Cara when they first became exclusive. She told Lindsay she didn't like the fact that Lindsay would be writing about some fictional characters she made up, then want to have sex with Cara soon after. Initially, she found it almost insulting, like Lindsay wasn't really thinking about her, but about the people she'd created. It took many in-depth conversations and countless reassurances, but Lindsay believed that Cara finally understood. Just because the writing got her juices flowing, that didn't mean Cara was some stand-in for who she really wanted to be with. It was nothing like that. In fact, it was far simpler —she was turned on and the only one she wanted to share that with was Cara.

Lindsay was young, but liked to think she was wise beyond her years when it came to making love to a woman. In her line of work, research and experimentation were key, and she was a very quick study. It made no sense to her for a writer of lesbian erotica not to be well-versed in the female form, how to read her, and how to please her. So she paid very close attention to everything she did to Cara and every reaction Cara had, good or bad. She knew when to take things slower (Cara's kisses weren't as deep). She knew when Cara wanted it fast and hard (Cara's pupils dilated and she fisted Lindsay's shirt in her hands). She knew when to relinquish the reins (Cara started on Lindsay's shirt before Lindsay could get to hers). And she knew when to take command because Cara would become putty in her hands, opening her body to Lindsay, letting her choose the direction they moved in.

Like now.

By the time the backs of Cara's legs hit the edge of the bed, Lindsay had her down to just panties, and those were removed in one swift maneuver. She lay completely naked on her back, vulnerable and trusting, a feast for Lindsay's eyes. Her skin was smooth and, her summer tan not completely faded yet, still a light brown. Sexy freckles dotted her shoulders, and her bare breasts were small and pert with dark nipples standing at attention. Lindsay moved her eyes downward, past the raspberry-shaped birthmark on Cara's tummy, past the roundness of her hips, to the thin, sandy-colored line of hair that Lindsay dubbed her "landing strip." When she looked back up, Cara was smiling at her.

"I love you," Cara said as Lindsay moved Cara's legs apart and draped them over her shoulders.

Lindsay lowered her head and inhaled deeply, taking in the essence, the musky tang of her beloved girlfriend. Using just the tip of her tongue, she sampled the salty-sweetness of the wet warmth. Cara sighed and Lindsay felt her thighs twitch under her hands. She turned her gaze back up to Cara, whose head was thrown back into the pillow in anticipation.

"Oh, baby, I love you too," Lindsay whispered.

Then she sank into paradise.

Cara White was tired. As she poured her fourth cup of coffee for the day, she shook her head, knowing she had nobody to blame but herself.

And Lindsay.

At the thought of her girlfriend and how they spent the night before, she smiled mischievously. They'd made love for hours, stopped to cook up a box of Kraft macaroni and cheese—naked. Then they ate it in bed as they shared the events of their day with each other. Then they made love some more. Cara remembered looking at the clock at 3:37 a.m. Her alarm was set for 7:00.

Yes, she was tired. She should know better than to disrupt her sleep the night before her long day at work; she was no longer a spring chicken. She was tired, but she was happy. And that thought surprised her.

When she and Lindsay first began dating, Cara honestly wasn't sure where it would go, how long it would last. And when she found out how much younger than her Lindsay actually was, Cara almost ran for the hills. But something stopped her...to this day, she still wasn't sure what it was. Lindsay's eyes that had a wise-beyond-her-years depth to them? Her open, generous heart and giving soul? The way she made love to Cara like no other woman ever had? Whatever it was, it kept Cara's feet planted firmly and made her stick things out to see where they'd go.

But she worried. Cara was pretty settled into her profession; Lindsay was still figuring out what she wanted to do with her life.

They had a blast together, but everybody knows that a relationship takes more than fun times.

Turned out, having fun with Lindsay was Cara's favorite thing in the world. They had a lot in common, the same wants in life and love even though they were in different places. Lindsay's writing seemed like a hobby at first, something she did on the side. But as she experimented with her work, evolved as a writer, and began to sell, began to actually make a name for herself, Cara started to understand that it was much more than a hobby. It was the path to becoming a career.

Cara had a tough time with that at first. Lindsay's stuff wasn't subtle. It wasn't discreet. It was bold, sometimes edgy, often raunchy, *always* graphic sex. And it made Cara uncomfortable. Especially the first time Lindsay went from writing a hot sex scene right into wanting to have sex with her. Cara totally freaked. Accused Lindsay of using her for her body and no other reason, accused her of wanting to be with her steamy characters rather than with Cara herself. They had a knock-down, drag-out fight that lasted well into the next day.

To Lindsay's credit, she hung in there. She explained over and over again that Cara was completely off-base. Yes, sometimes Lindsay's writing was a turn-on, but it was only the catalyst for wanting to be with Cara. She said it a hundred different ways and Cara finally forced herself to let go of any suspicions and to simply trust her girlfriend.

It wasn't easy, but she did it.

Thank god, because Lindsay was amazing, they made a fantastic couple, and the sex was spine-melting.

An impish grin on her face, Cara doctored her coffee with more sugar than she should and enough cream to sustain a starving cat and took a sip just as her coworker, Michael, came into the break room.

"Hey, why don't you have some coffee with your cream?" he asked her.

"Ha! That just never gets old, no matter how many times you use it," she replied wryly.

"How was your night?" He pulled a bottle of water out of the refrigerator.

"Awesome. Yours? Did you meet up with Mr. Six-Pack Abs?"

"I met up, down, and sideways with him. I swear to god, the man's a contortionist." He took a slug of his water, then said, "Speaking of hot monkey sex, didn't you spend the night with your little smut writer?"

"I did. And it's erotica, thank you very much."

"Smut. Erotica. Same thing." Michael reached down and poked one of Cara's thighs with a finger. "Sore?"

She laughed and slapped his hand away. "Yes, if you must know."

"Good." He waved a hand in a circle, encompassing her face. "You have dark circles under your eyes, but you're smiling. A good combination. I like it. Looks good on you."

Cara just smiled at him. She and Michael had been friends for nearly a decade, having started work the same week. While she worked more on clients with chronic pain, he leaned toward the terminally ill. There were days when talking and joking about their sex lives was the only way they could keep from dissolving into tears. That they ended up trusted friends was simply a bonus.

"Who's up next?" he asked, running a hand over his very short blonde hair.

Cara grimaced. "The Republican."

Michael made a face. "Ugh. Give him a Charlie horse."

"Don't tempt me."

Cara divided her clients into three general categories: the confessors, the conversationalists, and the stony silent types. Her mood determined how she felt about each category on any given day. The conversationalists were the most bearable. They were clients who would make a little small talk, but just enough to fill the room if silence felt at all uncomfortable. If Cara was tired like today, the stony silent clients could make an hour feel like five. Having time to be lost in her own thoughts wasn't a bad thing…unless she was in danger of falling asleep, mid-rub. If she was feeling prickly or irritated for any reason, the confessors could drive her up the wall. People had no idea that being a massage therapist was shockingly similar to being a bartender in that the confessors felt it necessary to spill their guts, to share with Cara their hopes, fears, dreams, beliefs. Maybe it was being face-down the majority of the time, not having to look her in the eye, that made them feel like they could unload. Cara knew infinitely more about most of her clients than she ever wanted to.

Judd Pierce had arthritis, so he had a standing weekly appointment with Cara. He was also a confessor. Cara and Michael dubbed him "The Republican" for obvious reasons. Inexplicably, Pierce felt that being on Cara's table was a green light to spout off on every government policy, every local politician, the president, and how "those idiot Democrats are running our country right into the shitter." Oftentimes, she'd tune him out and fantasize about telling him he was being massaged by a real live homosexual. Then she'd daydream about telling him all the homosexual places her hands have been, all the homosexual things they've done. More than once, she failed to stifle a giggle and had to fake a coughing jag to cover it up.

If Pierce wasn't a weekly, paying appointment, she'd seriously consider firing him as a client. But regulars were good for business, so she tolerated him.

At the front desk, she took a glance at her remaining day's schedule. Pierce was the only fly in the ointment of a decent day. Seeing the name of her last client brought a smile to her lips. Starting down the hall to get the room set up for The Republican, she figured she might as well get his appointment over with.

***

Judd Pierce actually lasted a good twenty minutes before the political ranting began about what a shitty job President Obama was doing.

"Election day can't come fast enough," he gruffed.

Cara wasn't even sure why she bothered with music during his session; it wasn't like he listened to it at all, and it certainly didn't seem to help him relax. Or her.

She didn't respond, just let him ramble on. She'd only needed one time to make the mistake of trying to actually converse with him about his views. She ended up so angry and frustrated, *she* needed a massage simply to help loosen the muscles that all felt like taut rubber bands after talking to him. Never again.

"I had Rush on this morning and…"

Cara rolled her eyes now as she dug her fingers into his calf muscle and prepared to tune him out. Rush Limbaugh was not somebody she needed to give one iota of thinking energy to. She wondered if Pierce realized how repetitive he was, how he sometimes managed to use the *exact same* sentences he'd used on her table last week. And the week before that. And the week before that. Deciding he most likely tortured each person he met with identical diatribes and then probably forgot who he'd already hit, Cara went into Zero Attention Mode, as she and Michael dubbed it. While Pierce blathered on, Cara let her thoughts drift to more pleasant topics.

Like last night with Lindsay.

Jesus.

Cara hadn't been kidding when she told Michael her thighs were sore; they were. Very sore. She lost track of how often or for how long she kept them apart. Or Lindsay held them apart. All Cara knew was she spent several hours flat on her back, soaking wet, and unendingly aroused. She had no idea how her young girlfriend had become such an amazing lover, but Cara knew they could never break up—Lindsay had pretty much ruined her for any other woman.

Cara's skin warmed, and she thanked god Pierce was face-down and couldn't see her expression of blissful satisfaction at the flashback. He was exactly the kind of guy who would make a comment. Then she'd be tempted to dig an elbow under his shoulder blade—or something equally as painful—and it would just be ugly all the way around. She took a deep breath and willed herself to calm down, to relax, to put all thoughts and memories of last night into a box and shelve them. For the time being.

When she finally finished with Pierce—who was still going on about impeachment—she covered him more with the sheet and quietly left the room so he could relax for the last few minutes of his time. And so she could do the same.

Michael passed her in the hall, asking in a stage whisper, "Are your ears bleeding?"

"You have no idea," she tossed over her shoulder as she entered the small office they shared.

Cara took some time to check her e-mail, fill out some paperwork, sign up for an upcoming seminar, drink a bottle of water, and munch on a handful of almonds. Her cell buzzed and she smiled as she opened a text from Lindsay that simply said, "Luv u." She smiled, both at the message and at the inability of her writer girlfriend to spell correctly when texting. She pulled in a deep, contented breath, let it out slowly, trying to remember when her life had ever felt so... right.

"Cara?" The voice on the intercom startled her.

"Yep."

"Your next appointment is here and ready for you."

"Okay. Thanks, Jeanne."

Cara finished her water, shot a text to Lindsay telling her she loved her too, and headed to the room where her client waited.

Geri Scott was a woman Cara had known for nearly twenty-five years. In fact, Geri had coached Cara's high school softball team. In her late fifties now, she owned her own landscape architecture company, which she built into a local success story. Luckily, she had a reliable staff of knowledgeable employees because her back couldn't take much more bending, lifting, or hauling, and she had to give up most of the jobs that required any kind of physical labor—not something that made her happy. She was another standing weekly appointment for Cara, but one she enjoyed much, much more than Judd Pierce.

Cara knocked on the door, then entered when permission was given.

"Hey there, Coach," Cara said quietly. "How's it going?"

"Good, Cara. Really good. You?"

"I'm great." Cara rubbed oil on her hands, moved the sheet draped over Geri's body, and went to work on her legs. She always did a full body massage even though the issues Geri had were centered on her back; working all the other muscles helped the overall well-being of the body. Geri was a small pit bull of a woman with close-cropped salt-and-pepper hair. Compact in size, she was solid and muscular. Her back problems were very difficult for her to deal with because they limited her ability to do the strenuous work she loved. "How's business?"

"Well, summer's over and fall will be on us before you know it, so things are winding down."

"But you like that," Cara said, remembering how tired Geri would get at the end of the summer, how her utter exhaustion would make her long for autumn.

"I do, though I don't relish it as much now that I'm not doing the hard stuff." Cara felt more than heard her chuckle.

"But your back is much happier. I guarantee it."

"That is very true. Things here okay?" Geri asked.

"Love it."

They made small talk, chatted about superficial things. Cara always found it interesting how they avoided any kind of conversation about their personal lives. Cara knew Geri had been living with the same woman—Ms. Hargrave, Cara's tenth-grade English teacher—for more than twenty years, and she was pretty sure Geri knew that she was family. She certainly didn't hide her life. But they never spoke of it. Cara chalked it up to a generational thing regarding what made appropriate conversation or not. Or maybe Geri still thought of Cara as a student and therefore not somebody she should converse with on a personal level. Cara didn't quite get it. For all the work Geri's generation had done to be recognized, why stay in the closet? Why not be out and proud?

It was only out of respect that Cara didn't force the subject somehow. Maybe she, too, still thought of Geri as her coach rather than a peer, and her parents raised her to be respectful of her elders, so she was.

Whatever. It was still silly as far as Cara was concerned; they were all adults. This was the twenty-first century, for god's sake. She thought about Lindsay, her very particular genre of writing, how hard it was for her to come out to her parents, and how honestly and openly she tried to live her life. A fierce wave of pride hit her and before she could stop herself, the question blurted out of her mouth.

"How's Ms. Hargrave?" Cara poured all her focus into continuing the massage, keeping her hands moving, knowing that if she stopped —even for a fraction of a second—she would devolve into a panic attack about how she stupidly overstepped her bounds.

"She's terrific," Geri said, without missing a beat. "Getting ready to retire in the next year or two, I think."

Cara's eyebrows shot up at the openness of the answer. "Good for her. She was a tough teacher, but one of my favorites."

"She's great at her job. And I'm pretty sure she'd say it's okay for you to call her Lisa now, you know."

Cara laughed. "I don't think I can," she said truthfully. "It seems… disrespectful." Cara thought back more than twenty years, remembered her English teacher, remembered looking at her legs way more often than she should have. "I had such a crush on her."

"Many of her students do," Geri replied, again not missing a beat.

"And you two have been together for how long?"

"Almost thirty years. My god, I can hardly believe it."

"Holy cow!"

"Right? Once time starts to speed up, it doesn't slow down." Her tone was wistful, almost dreamy.

"My mother is always saying the same thing."

"Your mother is right."

"I'll tell her you said so." Cara paused. "Thirty years. Wow. That's almost my whole life."

Geri snorted. "Yeah, thanks for the reminder."

With a laugh, Cara apologized, at the same time, trying to imagine being with Lindsay thirty years from now. She'd be sixty-seven. Jesus, that was hard to fathom. She shook her head and came back to the present.

"How about you?" Geri asked.

"Me?"

"You have somebody?"

"I do. Lindsay. She's a writer."

"Nice. How'd you meet?"

Cara was surprised at the genuine curiosity in the question. Geri really wanted to know. What was more, Cara wanted to tell. Why hadn't they ever talked like this before?

She told the story of the party where she first met Lindsay, working steadily on Geri's muscles as she did so. She could feel Geri chuckle here and there, especially when she mentioned the fourteen year age difference between them.

"I imagine you could teach her a thing or two," Geri teased.

"Believe me when I tell you, *she's* teaching *me*. It's totally bizarre."

"Even better."

When their laughter died down, the natural lull in the conversation allowed Cara to change the subject. "And how's the back been?" She focused on the inch-long scar at the small of Geri's back, a testament to the surgery she had two years ago to repair a herniated disk.

"Not too bad." Geri groaned as Cara worked the muscles in that area. "I try to avoid the muscle relaxants if I can because they knock me on my ass, but I do have to take them every so often. Overall, though, it's been okay. I've been following the orders of my massage therapist and I've been careful not to overdo it."

"That's what I like to hear." She dug her fingers into the tissue, working the tension out, visualizing the toxins leaving the muscles. "Not everybody listens to my suggestions."

"I didn't say suggestions. I said orders."

Cara could hear the smile in Geri's tone. "Careful. I can hurt you, you know."

The conversation quieted as Cara focused on the flesh beneath her hands, kneading, pushing, pressing, feeling the tissue shift, the knots dissipate. She paid close attention to the sound of Geri's breathing, using it to gauge when she should use more or less pressure. This was what she loved most about her job: she knew she was helping. She was making a difference in somebody's life. The human body was an amazing machine, one that Cara had no hope of ever understanding completely, but she did her best to learn the newest sciences and massage techniques in order to best serve her clients. Geri would leave this room feeling better than she did when she arrived and Cara played a big part in that. It was a satisfying feeling that filled her with pride. She couldn't imagine having any other career.

Finished with her work, she gently covered Geri back up and laid her hand on the small of her client's back.

"All set," she said softly. "You can lie here for as long as you'd like. Jeanne will make your next appointment for you on your way out." As an afterthought, she added, "Tell Ms. Hargrave—Lisa—I said hello."

Quietly, she left the room and headed toward her office.

She had the sudden urge to call Lindsay.

THE LANDSCAPE ARCHITECT

Geri Scott was not aging gracefully. She was fighting it every step of the way and it was really starting to piss her off. Her body was falling apart, or so it seemed to her. She couldn't lift things like she used to; any time she tried, her back pain stabbed through her like she'd been punctured with an ice pick. Nearly thirty years of sports—including softball, field hockey, and basketball—did her knees in for good. They snapped and popped like bubble wrap whenever she attempted to squat. Now she needed help back up to a standing position. And now the knuckles in her hands were beginning to ache.

It was all so unfair.

Her old man bequeathed her the arthritis, of that Geri was sure. Recalling her father made her drift off into her own thoughts as, alone in the room with Cara gone, she relaxed on the massage table. Geri also inherited her father's work ethic and his love of working with his hands. Tom Scott was a mason in his heyday, a good one. He taught his only daughter that there was no work more honest than good, hard, physical labor. He loved it, and so did she. Geri's fondest memories were of helping her father build things. Together, they made the shelves that still hung in the living room of the family home, the picnic table in her parents' back yard as well as the one she had in her own, and the hutch that held her mother's good china. When she began cultivating an interest in landscape architecture, he helped her design the front of her parents' house, her grandparents' house, her Uncle Jim's house, and her own.

Sometimes, it was hard to watch him work. He moved so much slower than she remembered, a painful reminder that he was no longer a young man, that she wouldn't have him forever. His knees were his biggest issue, which meant, of course, that he used his back much more often than he should for lifting. Geri tried to keep a close eye on him and not let him lift things he shouldn't, but she missed a lot. More importantly, he hated being made to feel old and frail, so he was not always grateful for help. More often than not, it made him downright cranky.

Geri Scott was a carbon copy of her father. She was only now beginning to realize it.

If only she could convince him to have a regular massage. Oh, he'd never go to Cara. A woman younger than his own kids touching him like that? No way. He was nothing if not old-fashioned and he'd find that all kinds of inappropriate. But Geri was sure Cara could recommend an older male massage therapist. Her dad wouldn't be cured, but he'd feel so much better, at least for a little while. She always did.

Sitting up slowly, she focused on her breathing the way Cara had instructed her. Her legs dangled over the side of the table as she took the time to feel each muscle group, flex them, stretch them. Though she knew it wouldn't last more than a couple of days, Geri felt almost like a new woman. It was this sensation that kept her coming back week after week, like the one beautiful drive in an otherwise crappy golf game that made you want to play another eighteen frustrating holes tomorrow, just in case you might hit it like that again.

Plus, she enjoyed Cara's company, liked talking to her. Surprised as she was by the direction today's conversation had gone, she wasn't the least bit uncomfortable. She'd pegged Cara as a dyke-in-the-making more than twenty years ago when she coached the girls' softball team. She and Lisa'd had a little betting pool going between the two of them. In the fifteen years Geri coached, she was eighteen for twenty. Not a bad record and a pretty solid testament to the fact that her gaydar was spot-on accurate. She was actually amazed the subject hadn't come up sooner, as Cara never seemed the type to not speak what was on her mind. Next time, Geri would have to take the lead, get the conversation started.

Dressed and relaxed, Geri headed out to the lobby and made her next appointment. She pocketed one of Cara's cards to remind her to call about her dad. Then she headed out to the red pickup with the company logo and set a course for Garrison's, a little nearby wine store. She had a hankering for something nice, maybe a soft, gentle red.

It was nearing six-thirty, so the after-work rush had already been and gone, a fact that pleased Geri. It was a small neighborhood store and when it was crowded, maneuvering through the aisles could make for a tight fit, but there was something about Garrison's that kept her coming back. It had been standing for decades, and once it was passed down, after his death, from David Garrison to his daughter Dorian, it was woman-owned—lesbian-owned, to be specific. Geri came in often enough that Dorian Garrison knew her by name. And despite being a good twenty years younger than Geri, Dorian knew her shit about wine. She was knowledgeable, approachable, and helpful.

And cute. Geri was a sucker for cute.

"Hey there, Ms. Scott," Dorian said with her usual hundred-watt smile as Geri approached the counter.

"Dorian, how many times have I told you to please call me Geri?"

A pretty pale pink flushed into Dorian's high cheekbones. "A few."

"A few dozen is closer to the truth."

"You're probably right." She leaned her forearms onto the counter and asked, "What can I help you with today?" The direct contact from her dark eyes allowed for many different interpretations of her tone, and Geri bit back a grin.

"Oh, such a loaded question," she cracked, then winked. "How about some wine?"

Dorian feigned disappointment and followed it up with a grin. "Fine. Wine will have to do." She came around the counter, asking, "What's for dinner?"

"I'm not sure," Geri admitted, "but I think I heard something about spaghetti this morning." She fell into step with Dorian as they walked the short distance to the red wine display. Dorian tapped her forefinger against her lips as she scanned the shelves. Geri took that moment to study her.

Her short dark hair was an explosion of tight curls over her small head, and she definitely had the bone structure to pull off such a style. Eyes as black as onyxes were accented by lashes and brows just as dark. Hammered silver earrings in an artsy, spiral shape dangled from her ears, but they were her only jewelry today. Her skin tone and hair texture always made Geri assume Dorian was biracial, but there never was a time that seemed right to ask such a personal question, so she just hadn't. She was a petite woman to begin with, about 5 foot 2 inches and no more than 110 pounds soaking wet, but Geri was certain Dorian had lost weight recently and had reached the point where she was almost too thin. Wondering whether the shedding of pounds was intentional or not, Geri was pulled from her thoughts when Dorian spoke.

"You smell great. Massage today?"

"Just finished one."

"I thought so. I think my cousin uses the same massage oil on his clients. I love it." She pulled a bottle down from the shelf without missing a beat, though Geri noticed an even deeper pink shadowing her cheeks.

Yup. Totally cute.

Handing the bottle to Geri, she said, "Try this one. I think Lisa will like it. It's a Pinot Noir, not too dry—I know she hates that. Tell her it's not too fruity, but it's fruity enough to keep her interested. A little vanilla, a hint of oak, maybe a little blackberry and cherry on the finish, but enough spice to keep it from venturing into sweetness."

"I will never remember all that," Geri said with a chuckle, "but I'll give it a try."

"Trust me."

"I always do."

They headed back to the counter, Geri with a slight limp that she assumed was undetectable.

"Still thinking about retiring?" Dorian asked. The store was quiet with only two other customers milling around. Geri was the only one at the counter.

"I'm sorry?"

Dorian glanced up at her. "Last time you were here, you said you'd started thinking about maybe retiring, since your back was giving you so much trouble. I see you're still limping a bit, so…" She trailed off and Geri could tell by her expression that she worried she'd overstepped her bounds. "I'm sorry. It's none of my business."

"No, no. You're fine." Geri rushed to reassure her. "No worries at all." She recalled her last visit was at the end of a particularly rough day. She'd lifted too much mulch, she'd spent too much time using a shovel, and it was rainy and damp, which didn't help the arthritis any. By the time she rolled into the store to cheer herself up with a nice bottle of Cabernet, she was in grueling pain and was seriously considering throwing in the towel on working. With a sigh, she said, "I don't know, Dorian. Could I retire? What would I do? I'd get up, have breakfast and read the paper. Then I'd watch *Kelly Live*. And then it's eleven in the morning and I'm done. My day would be over. What do I do after that?"

Dorian's gentle laughter lifted her shoulders up and down. She said, "My Uncle Derek retired last year. He used to say exactly the same thing you just did and you know what? I see him less now than I did when he was working. He's so busy! It's ridiculous. You'd find things to occupy your time. I'm sure of it. And more importantly, you'd be giving your body a better chance to heal."

"I suppose you're right." Geri exhaled a frustrated breath and paid.

"I am once in a while."

They said their goodbyes and Geri headed home, her mind on what Dorian said and remembering how she felt during that last trip when her body was aching so badly she could barely stand long enough to pay for her alcohol. She was infinitely more mobile when she wasn't working. When she and Lisa took a week's vacation, Geri felt terrific by the end of the seven days. After two days back at work, she was aching again.

Stubbornness ran in Geri's family. She knew that. She was very much an if-you-want-it-done-right-do-it-yourself kind of girl. She learned that from her dad. Unfortunately, doing it all herself was becoming less and less of an option, and it was soon going to be time for her to deal with that.

God, she hated getting old.

She was right about the spaghetti, the house permeated with the mouth-watering aroma of Lisa's homemade sauce. Geri followed her nose to the kitchen where her partner of nearly three decades stood at the counter in the apron Geri gave her for Christmas a few years ago. *Smooth, sophisticated, full-bodied. And the wine's not bad, either,* it read in bold white letters on a burgundy fabric. Geri wrapped her arms around Lisa as she chopped veggies for a salad.

"Hi, babe."

"Hey, you." Lisa turned her head and pecked Geri on the lips. "How was the massage?"

"Very nice, as always." Geri snatched a cherry tomato and popped it into her mouth. "By the way, Cara White had a crush on you in tenth grade English."

"Really? And is the sky blue, too?"

"I figured you probably knew."

"Fifteen-year-olds are not exactly known for their subtlety."

"True."

"And she was a cute little baby dyke. She stood out to me."

Geri smiled against Lisa's hair and handed her the wine. "I brought you a present. Dorian says you'll love it."

"A Pinot, huh?"

"Yup. She said a bunch of other things too, but I don't remember them. You'll love it. That's all I can come up with."

"She has yet to steer me wrong," Lisa commented, and it was true. "How long until dinner?"

"You've got about twenty minutes. Go shower off the oil." With another kiss, Lisa sent Geri on her way.

Something akin to melancholy settled over Geri as she walked through the house—the life—she'd built with Lisa. It wasn't an entirely unpleasant feeling, but it made her more cerebral, more pensive about the current path of her life and what her immediate future might hold. Lisa had been trying to get her to retire for almost two years now. *Soon* was always Geri's answer, though *soon* never seemed to get any closer.

She passed down the hallway slowly, stopping to look at each photograph Lisa had hung lovingly, precisely, on the wall. They were excerpts of their life together, like still shots from a movie. Their trip to Ireland more than twenty years ago, both smiling, intoxicated, and looking impossibly young. The two of them sitting in front of their first Christmas tree, a pathetic sapling that made Charlie Brown's tree look full and mature. Geri grinned as she thought about Lisa pleading to let her get that one, that it was just too small and sad to be left at the garden store, how nobody would buy it and how no tree should be left all alone at Christmas. Geri hadn't stood a chance against that face of hers, the pleading eyes, the pouty lips. The tree had one sturdy branch on it, so that's where all their ornaments were hung. They looked stupidly happy sitting there on Christmas morning in their jammies in front of what was essentially a decorated branch. And again, unbearably young.

"Were we really such babies?" she whispered to the air.

Continuing down the hall, Geri's gaze skimmed over snapshots of her life, a bittersweet sigh escaping as she passed the pictures of the five different dogs they'd chosen, loved, and lost in their time together, finally deciding they couldn't take the heartbreak one more time. It was still weird to come home and not be greeted by a wet nose and wagging tail. More photos, more memories, and not for the first time, Geri understood how lucky she was. Like any long-term couple, she and Lisa had their bumps, their issues, their heated arguments. They had ugly moments and they each said things at one time or another that they wish they hadn't. But ultimately, they were there for one another with a strong, deep love and gentle forgiveness that outlasted any kind of muck, no matter how thick. Geri couldn't imagine her life without Lisa. And more than anything, what she did *not* want was for Lisa to have to take care of her down the road. With her back issues and her arthritis, she knew she could end up at least somewhat disabled if she didn't watch herself, if she wasn't more careful and less stubborn.

She shucked her clothes and stepped into the hot shower. Standing so the water tattooed a gentle rhythm on her back, she braced herself against the wall and inhaled deeply. "God, I can't stand getting older," she muttered into the steam. The thought of being weak, of not being able to carry her own weight, nearly brought her to her knees. If she was anything, Geri was independent.

A quick wash and rinse and she was finished. At the dresser in the bedroom, yet another shot of her and Lisa—this time on an Olivia cruise to Alaska—looked out at her from a brushed silver frame; their faces radiated warmth and happiness. When she picked up the picture and looked closer, one corner of Geri's mouth quirked up as if tugged by an invisible thread.

Do we always look this happy? she wondered as she rubbed her short hair with a towel.

The thought flushed a lovely tenderness through her entire being and an answer to her question seemed to come to her from nowhere and everywhere at once.

Yes. Because we are.

Nodding slowly, she set the photo frame back down and glanced around the room, the most important room in the house, in her life. The walls were soft khaki, the accents eggplant and ivory. She and Lisa picked the colors together; Lisa stumbled across the paisley print bed linens and matching curtains when shopping with her mother one day. She found them totally by accident. The hardwood was polished to a glorious shine and the area rug was thick and plush. They shared everything in this room: sleep and dreams, emotional meltdowns, lovemaking (both gentle and raw), favorite TV shows, foot rubs, favorite books, endless conversation. It was the heart of their home and for some reason, standing in the middle of it, completely naked and still damp from her shower, Geri Scott finally got it.

Lisa was just untying her apron when Geri came in from cleaning up. "Good timing. Everything's ready."

"Smells delicious," Geri said, taking Lisa in her arms and kissing her more intimately and thoroughly than usual, more than she had in a while.

When she was freed and fighting a slight flush, Lisa arched one eyebrow and studied Geri. "What was that for?"

"What? Can't I kiss my wife?" She winked at Lisa and grabbed the bottle of wine that was now breathing on the counter. "*Vino?*"

"You better believe it."

With a nod, Geri poured two glasses. They took their places at the table where Geri held her glass up to toast.

Lisa tilted her head slightly, waiting.

"I love you so much," Geri said softly. "To us." She touched her glass to Lisa's.

"I love you too."

They dug in, Geri eating slowly, wanting to savor the deliciousness of Lisa's cooking. After a few bites, she said nonchalantly, "I think it's time for me to retire."

Lisa's gaze snapped up and she blinked several times, her fork stopped in mid-air halfway to her mouth. She watched Geri's face and Geri wondered what she was searching for. Dishonesty? Teasing? Insanity? Geri simply looked back at her and said again, "I think it's time."

An interesting mix of elation, fear, and relief blended together and spread itself across Lisa's face. She pursed her lips like she was thinking, then gave a nod and took the bite of dinner. Chewing slowly, she never took her eyes from Geri. She swallowed, sipped her wine, and gave one more nod.

"Okay. Let's talk."

THE WINE SHOP OWNER

For the first night in nearly a month, Dorian Garrison finished tallying up the days' totals and did *not* end up with a massive headache. She actually had a somewhat decent day of business, something that was not happening nearly often enough lately. A large local grocery-store chain had opened a huge warehouse-type liquor store not two miles from her shop. Another long-standing liquor store had expanded, and now she could fit five of her shops into the middle of theirs and still have room to spare. It was getting harder and harder to compete, and she recently had to face one nausea-inducing fact.

It was very possible she was going to lose her business.

Soon.

This year.

The front door locked and the closed sign facing out, Dorian stood in the glass door and watched the street outside. It was a good location. Frankly, that's probably what kept her afloat for this long. Lots of foot traffic, lots of shoppers from other nearby stores made for spontaneous pop-in customers. A gourmet ice cream parlor was lit up across the street in pink and blue neon, people bustling about, despite the beginnings of fall in the air. A coffee shop next to it housed young urban professionals, college students, and gay couples. Soft strains of piano music could be heard through the wall of her shop coming from the upscale restaurant next door. It was a great street that was only improving as time went on. Her father had chosen the spot well.

Owning the building was also a blessing. There was no way she'd be able to afford the rent in this neighborhood, not for the storefront she had now, all big windows right in the center of the action. Her financial advisor suggested she could collect a nice chunk of change in rent if she were to close the wine shop and rent the storefront out to another business...and she knew he was right. But the thought of letting go of something that her father had built from the ground up, something he'd put his heart and soul into, was too much to bear right now. No, she was determined to hold on as long as she possibly could.

Besides, she loved wine. *Loved* it. She loved the color, the smell, the taste, the personality of it, the way each bottle told a story of its maker, of the land it came from, of the soil in which the grapes grew. Nothing was more mysterious, more romantic, than a good bottle of wine as far as Dorian was concerned, and people either got that or they didn't.

Her last girlfriend didn't.

The woman she was dating now—it was much too early in the relationship to call her a girlfriend—didn't either.

Letting out a tired breath, Dorian turned away from the front of the darkened store. On the way past the shelves, she slid down a bottle of the Pinot Noir she'd sent home with Geri Scott, and took it with her to the door in the back corner of the store. The door was painted the same color as the wall and if you didn't know it was there, you'd probably miss it. Behind it was a narrow flight of stairs that led up to the surprisingly roomy apartment that Dorian called home.

"Hi, Spike," she said affectionately to the white cat that wound itself around her ankles, meowing plaintively, telling her in cat-speak that it was well past his dinner time. She jotted a quick note to herself to remember to take the bottle of Pinot into account when tallying inventory in the morning, and left it on the round bistro table tucked into the corner of the small kitchen. Yes, she loved wine, but she was not so irresponsible that she just helped herself to the store's inventory without docking herself for it. Her father would have laughed at her being such a stickler, but she was determined. If her business was going to go under, it wasn't going to be because the owner was helping herself to the goods and not keeping track.

The open windows in the living room let in a wonderfully tepid evening breeze, carrying with it the smell of autumn and the sound of the people on the street below, and for a short moment, her brain began to calculate sales if only two of every ten people came in and bought a bottle of wine. Quickly, she shook the thoughts free. Before they could make her crazy, which they would. And had in the past. Yes, she could stay open later. In fact, she used to stay open until 9:00 every weeknight as well as Saturdays, but not without consequence: complete and utter exhaustion on her part.

No, it was infinitely smarter for her to close early a couple of nights a week. Not as profitable, but smarter, at least until she could afford to hire back the two assistants she had to lay off three months ago. Or hire people like them, as she was reasonably sure they weren't sitting at home twiddling their thumbs and waiting for her call. She hated having to let them go. They were good workers, friends, one of them having been with her father for ten years prior to Dorian's taking over the shop. But financially, she just couldn't justify keeping them on. It broke her heart and the guilt still ate at her if she dwelled too long. She did what she had to do to keep the business alive. And it sucked.

Dorian made short work of the cork in the Pinot and poured herself a glass. She swirled it around, watched the rich crimson leave legs on the glass, catch the light, and throw it back. Her dad used to tell her that the simple act of watching wine in a decent wine glass would calm his nerves and ease his soul. Dorian would laugh at him, tell him he'd obviously consumed too much of his product...until the day of his funeral.

It was the first time in her life she'd felt the weight of utter devastation.

It was also the first time she'd actually, honestly understood her father's connection to wine. She'd survived the day—she still wasn't quite sure how—and once alone, she'd opened a bottle of his favorite Zin. As she poured it into one of his crystal glasses, she felt as if somebody was also pouring peace into her aching heart. It sounded so incredibly corny that she'd never shared it with anybody. Ever. But that didn't keep it from being true. Since that moment, she'd felt as if, somehow, her father was still with her, still keeping an eye on her, still loving her, and she'd vowed to do everything in her power to keep his legacy alive.

Only now it was failing. *She* was failing, and it was crushing her.

"I miss you, Daddy," she whispered to the empty room, holding up her wine in salute.

A quiet buzz indicated an incoming text and Dorian grabbed her iPhone.

Know it's your early nite. Feel like company?

"Oh, Gina," Dorian sighed.

Torn. That's how she felt so often—too often—when it came to Gina.

The thought of her now, all dark hair, olive skin, and soft eyes, gently soothed Dorian. All she had to do was text back and tell her to come over. She'd be there in under twenty minutes. She'd sit on the couch and coax Dorian's head into her lap, and she'd stroke her forehead, scratch her scalp, smooth away all the stress and worry. Gina's mere presence could be a balm for Dorian's aching existence. Who cared if they didn't have a ton in common or if Gina—despite being Italian—didn't like wine? She was good company and Dorian didn't have to be alone.

So why couldn't she just send the text?

Since she could no longer afford to continue paying, she'd stopped seeing her therapist for the time being, but Dorian knew what she'd say. Guilt, first and foremost. Dorian felt guilty for not being able to keep her father's business as successful as he had. She felt like she was failing his memory and herself and because of that, she felt she didn't deserve anything good. Like Gina. So she would punish herself by not seeing Gina as often as she could, as often as she wanted to, as often as she *needed* to. But there was also an element of being picky—or too picky, as her best friend continually pointed out. Was that really so bad, though? Why was it a bad thing to know exactly what she wanted and to be willing to wait for it, even when something— acceptable—was within reach?

A chuckle escaped Dorian's throat as she realized it was a good thing she wasn't trying to pay her therapist because she obviously didn't need one. The chuckle died as she remembered the one thing she did need, at least for a while.

"Shit. I forgot to get my prescription filled." Spike looked up from his perch on the window sill, his big, green eyes boring into her as if he understood everything she said. Dorian crossed to him and scratched behind his ears, about the only place she was allowed to scratch without him scratching her back. And not in a good way. "I'll be right back. Okay, big guy?"

Bag slung across her body, she descended the back staircase and was out onto the street and into the noise and moving bodies, the complete opposite of the peace of her little apartment.

Dorian Garrison was well-known in the neighborhood, first as the daughter of David Garrison, the wine-shop owner, then as the owner herself. People nodded their greetings as she passed; everybody had a smile for her and she did her best to smile back. Three blocks down the street was Joe's Drugs, another privately-owned shop that had been on the street for decades. Dorian wondered if Joe went through the same issues she did, wondered if the Walgreen's and Rite Aids of the country were keeping him awake at night, questioning the survival of his business. She patronized Joe's for that exact reason: Why should she expect anybody to buy from her small business if she didn't do the same for other small businesses?

Joe's was fairly busy for a weeknight. Busier than her shop was, that's for sure. A half-dozen customers milled around, browsing shelves, as Dorian walked to the back counter where the pharmacy lived.

"Hi, Ms. Garrison." Liv, one of the two pharmacists Joe employed, smiled at Dorian and this time, Dorian smiled back with a completely genuine expression. Liv was adorable and sweet, and she was another reason Dorian preferred to visit Joe's for her prescriptions. She hated being on anti-anxiety meds, but she loved that she had an excuse to see Liv once a month. "How's the wine business?"

"Eh. It's there. Doing the best I can in this crappy economy."

"I know exactly what you mean. They say an upturn is on its way." She held up her hand and intertwined her first two fingers. "Fingers crossed."

Dorian did the same. "Mine too." Pulling her pill bottle out of her bag, she said, "I need a refill, please."

"You got it."

Dorian moved to her right a bit, making a show of studying the over-the-counter cold medicines, but in actuality, she was watching Liv as she worked behind the high counter. Her light brown hair was caught in a simple braid, the end resting just between her shoulder blades, and even under the store's harsh fluorescent lights, it seemed glossy and soft. Black-rimmed, rectangular glasses framed gentle brown eyes, and she wore very little—if any—makeup. Adorable freckles decorated the pale, smooth skin of her face. Deep dimples punctuated her cheeks. Her white lab coat could be a size smaller, as it seemed to engulf her torso, swallowing what Dorian suspected were some very nice curves. She wasn't at all overweight, not to Dorian. She was...full-figured? *Would that be the politically correct phrase?* Dorian wondered. Liv was simply larger than the stick figures today's society deemed perfect. *Hell, aren't we all?* Dorian thought and almost scoffed aloud. Liv had a beautifully feminine roundness to her—ample hips, full breasts, a nice behind—and Dorian found it all immensely appealing. She suspected Liv was one of those women who had no idea how attractive she really was, maybe even worried about her weight, and that made Dorian a little sad for her. She was an utterly pleasant person, warm and comfortable to be around; Dorian suspected that was a major reason Joe hired her. She drew people to her, made them feel at ease and relaxed.

Liv also patronized the wine shop on several occasions and Dorian really liked that. She seemed to know the basics of wine and was always interested in learning more; she asked questions and took recommendations well.

And she pinged Dorian's gaydar in a pretty significant way.

As if reading her thoughts, Liv called to her and asked, "Do you remember that Malbec you sold me a couple of weeks ago?"

"The Argentinean one. Did you like it?"

"I loved it. I took it to my cousin's dinner party and the whole place raved about it."

"Excellent."

"We got talking about wine and different varieties and what we each liked and didn't. My cousin is in marketing and we started batting around ideas about increasing our business if we owned a wine store. He came up with some great suggestions and I thought maybe you and I could sit down and go over them, just for fun." She stopped suddenly and cleared her throat, as if worried she'd crossed a line. "Um..."

Dorian blinked at her, unable to think of anything other than how adorable Liv looked with her cheeks all flushed pink.

"Like classes," Liv continued, picking up speed. "You know so much about wine and I know there are a ton of people like me who would like to learn more. So you could charge, like, twenty or thirty bucks a head for a two-hour class in your shop at night or something like that, and I bet you'd bring in a bunch of interested parties." She took a breath, pressed her lips together and kept them that way.

A grin broke out on Dorian's face. "I love that idea," she said, and it was true.

A relieved breath escaped Liv's lips—her full, incredibly kissable lips—and she let go of a nervous laugh. "Wow. That was really presumptuous of me." She handed Dorian her pills. "I apologize."

"Don't," Dorian said as she paid. "Please don't. I'd love to hear more of your ideas."

"You would?"

"Absolutely."

"You're open tomorrow?"

"I'm open all the time," Dorian said wryly. "The curse of owning a small shop."

Liv's smile lit up her entire face, crinkling the corners of her eyes in a way that made Dorian itch to touch them, to smooth them with her thumb. "I don't work until late tomorrow afternoon. I'll stop by before?"

"That would be great. I've got a new Chardonnay I'd like your opinion on."

Liv's grin widened. "You got it."

For the first time in her life, Dorian completely understood the phrase about your steps being lighter. She felt like she walked on air all the way back to her apartment. Back upstairs, she swooped Spike into her arms, much to his very vocal dismay, and spun him around like a dance partner.

"I think I just asked her out, Spikey." She stopped twirling and tilted her head like a dog listening to a far-off sound. "Or did she ask me out?" She kissed the cat's furry white head. "It came out of nowhere. All of a sudden, she just started rambling on. I've never seen her do that in all the time I've been going there. What if all this time I've been checking her out using my peripheral vision, she's been doing the same? How cool is that?"

Spike had enough, and he used his claws and legs to push out of Dorian's arms. It did nothing to deter her excitement.

"Not only did she ask me out—I think—but she has ideas for the store." Dorian picked up the half-empty glass of Pinot from the counter where she'd left it and took a healthy sip. Then she stared off into space for long moments, just absorbing the day, the hour, the minute. "I don't know what will happen, Spikey, but for this moment? Right now? I feel good. I'm going to hold on to that for a while."

Her iPhone sat next to the open wine bottle. Dorian picked it up and texted Gina.

Thanks, but I'm going to call it an early night.

She hit send and didn't feel the least bit bad about it.

THE PHARMACIST

Olivia Keegan loved her job. Not the drug part of it as much as the people part of it. She was a total people person, and she adored nothing more than visiting with new folks and answering their questions, being able to contribute even the smallest amount of help that might allow them to feel better. It made her day, her week, her month, her year. Hell, it made her life. Liv was born to serve and she loved it.

She had her favorites and her least favorites as far as customers went, and she enjoyed being the pharmacist at a small, neighborhood store. She knew she could find a job at a larger chain in a heartbeat—and make quite a bit more money. But the customers at Joe's were loyal. They knew Liv and Liv knew them. That familiarity was something she wasn't willing to give up, not even for more money in her paycheck.

Dorian Garrison was definitely a favorite of Liv's. Cute and charming, Liv was sure Dorian flirted with her a little bit and Liv flirted right back. Well, as much as Liv could manage to flirt; it certainly wasn't her strong point. Although tonight...good god, what happened? She actually, sort of, pretty much asked Dorian out. Almost. Didn't she? Was popping by the shop to talk about wine and marketing considered a date? Maybe. And if Liv wasn't mistaken, Dorian seemed...happy about it. She said yes, after all. And she smiled. Widely. Adorably. Liv tried not to wonder why somebody as confident as independent as Dorian Garrison would be at all interested in somebody like Liv, but she'd take it where she could get it. It's not like she had dates lining up outside her door.

Her best friend, Danny, would tell her that was her own fault. Danny had as many men in his life as Liv did *not* have women. Liv could almost hear his voice now. *You need to put yourself out there, Livvy. You need to go out, go to parties and gatherings, make yourself available, get noticed. Ms. Right isn't going to just knock on your front door one day, you know.* Liv did know. Danny was one hundred percent right and Liv did know that. But knowing something and making it happen were two very different things. She wished she had an eighth of Danny's confidence. How did gay men do it? She could be walking through the mall with Danny, he would make eye contact with some guy across the floor, excuse himself from her, and go get a hand job in the men's room. Not that that was the kind of female contact Liv wanted, but she could barely figure out how to find a date, while Danny was having random sex in every public place imaginable. There was a little part of her that was totally jealous.

The main store lights clicked off and Liv heard Joe, Jr., the son of the original Joe and now the owner, locking the front doors. Her pharmacy area remained lit as she did some final counts and checked her computer to make sure things were clearly set up for Glen, the other pharmacist at Joe's. He had the morning shift this week. He and Liv traded back and forth, one opening, the other closing for a week. Then they'd switch. It could be exhausting, but it worked. There was also a part-time pharmacist who took weekends and some nights so Liv and Glen could take vacation or whatever.

"All set, Olivia?" Joe called from the greeting-card aisle.

"Just about." She finished up, hung her white coat on the coat tree in the corner and exchanged it for a windbreaker, and unlocked the bottom drawer to retrieve her bag. Her cell phone showed a text from Danny.

Come to Black. Buy you a Cosmo.

"Ugh." The last thing in the world Liv felt like was going to a dark club with pounding house music and weak drinks. At thirty-three, she thought she was past that kind of night out, but Danny loved it. The only way she could drag him to the occasional foreign film or poetry reading was if she accompanied him to Black once in a while. "Not tonight," she said aloud. She had a cat, a couch, and the latest Nora Roberts novel all calling her name.

She sent a quick text back declining the invite, then turned her sound down, knowing Danny's next move would be to call her and beg. After that, he'd resort to trying to guilt her into going. She didn't want to deal with any of it. She just wanted to go home. She bid her goodnights to Joe and left.

***

Liv's apartment wasn't much bigger than the too-small dance floor at Black, but it was much more comfortable for her, despite the pang she got every time she entered the front door and realized nobody was waiting for her or coming over later. She was alone and would be for the night. The zap of loneliness was much easier to handle than it had been, but it still had some sting.

Diane left nearly eight months ago. To Liv, it felt like it was ten years on some days. On others, it was as fresh as if it happened yesterday. Today fell somewhere in between, and not for the first time, she was thankful they hadn't lived together, that they'd kept their own places. It was hard enough to deal with the empty spaces left by Diane's coffee maker, her craft beer, her toothbrush; thank god there hadn't been furniture, pets, or kids to split. Even though the few items Diane did leave were all temporary items, it was simply too painful to keep any of them around, so much so that she couldn't even bring herself to give the useful items away. She threw it all out. Every last thing. If Diane decided she'd rather be with some other woman, then that other woman could sure as shit buy her the things she wanted. Liv certainly had.

Dropping her keys on the small table by the door as she passed, Liv hung up her jacket and headed toward the narrow galley kitchen. Lunch felt like forever ago, and her empty stomach made itself known. The fridge's contents looked like they belonged to somebody with a split personality. Yogurt, salad fixings, skim milk, tofu, cheddar, heavy cream, half a chocolate cheesecake, butter. Liv shook her head. That's what she did on the days that she actually recognized the dichotomy of her personality: she shook her head in dismayed wonder. She almost *was* two different people, thanks to Diane. The majority of the time, she was self-conscious and hated her body. She was overweight, unattractive, out of shape, and had no fashion sense. The tiny remainder of the time, she focused on trying to accept herself and just be happy with who she was—a woman overweight, unattractive, out of shape, and with no fashion sense.

Liv's self-confidence was never a solid part of her, but Diane's infidelity shattered it completely. Liv was aware of the effect such a thing had on a person's psyche and she tried to cut herself a little slack, but it wasn't easy, not when she was already so critical of herself and her appearance. She was a good girlfriend. Liv knew that. She was kind, loving, giving, supportive. So if Diane didn't want to be with her—if Diane wanted to be with somebody else *instead* of her—it had to be about Liv physically. Didn't it? It never occurred to her that Diane's inability to be faithful was about nothing other than Diane.

It had taken a good four months of therapy to figure that one out.

Truth was, Liv actually had taken a step toward—she hoped— feeling better about her body and because of it, she pulled lettuce, celery, a cucumber, and a tomato out of the refrigerator. As she poured herself a glass of Chardonnay, Chloe, her calico cat, wandered into the room and twined around Liv's ankles like an anaconda.

"Oh, sure. You hear the front door and you couldn't care less. You hear the *refrigerator* door and poof. Here you are. Nice."

Chloe meowed and sat, staring up at Liv with green eyes that seemed almost human at times.

"What am I? Chopped liver?" Liv asked as she tore lettuce into a bowl.

Chloe meowed again, this time adding a paw on Liv's calf with just enough claw to get some attention.

"I know, I know," Liv said, wiping her hands on a towel. "But first? Love." She swooped Chloe up in her arms amid loud, yet somehow half-hearted, protests. "Yeah, yeah. It's terrible to be loved by me. My kisses and hugs are awful, aren't they?" She held the cat close, nuzzled her, and scratched under her chin, a seemingly favorite spot. Within seconds, the gentle vibrating began and Liv smiled. "Got your purr on, I see." She held the cat for long moments, enjoying the warmth of a living body snuggled close. When she finally opened the refrigerator door, Chloe seemed to gain new life, struggling to get down, then waiting anxiously by her bowl.

"So predictable," Liv said as she poured cream into the bowl. "Only a little bit. I don't want you to get fat like me." As soon as the words were out of her mouth, she could hear her own twelve-year-old voice scolding her mother, who had many variations of the same put-downs. *Mom, stop it. Why do you always say that? You're not fat. You're beautiful and I love you.*

The fruit doesn't fall far from the tree. Isn't that what they say?

Liv finished making her salad, refilled her wine glass, and took both into the living room where she made herself comfortable on the chocolate brown couch. Liv was a huge fan of earthiness—whether it be color, smell, or feel—and she'd decorated her apartment in that vein. The walls were painted a comforting olive green, which complemented the dark wood trim perfectly. Gleaming hardwood floors made it feel bigger than it actually was and matching area rugs in beiges and burgundies added to the ambiance. Much as Liv hated the cold weather, winter was her favorite season in her apartment. She'd click on the gas fireplace, curl up under an afghan with a good book, and just lose herself in warmth and comfort. Maybe one of these days, she'd have somebody new on whose lap she could rest her feet on such days.

Dorian Garrison's perhaps?

Shaking the thought away, she crunched on a forkful of salad as she watched Chloe saunter into the room and go to work on her scratching post. Liv was lucky with Chloe, especially since she adopted her from the Humane Society at three years old and did not have a lot of info about what she'd be bringing home. Chloe never scratched up any of the furniture, crapped in any of Liv's shoes, or peed on any clothes. She stayed off the kitchen counter—though she did like the sideboard because it was in front of a window. She even cuddled on occasion, though it was always on her terms. She was good company and Liv was thankful to have another living being in the apartment with her. By her estimation, if she was talking to the cat, she wasn't talking to herself.

Finished with her salad, she set the empty bowl on the end table and her eye was caught by the pamphlet she'd left there. Opening the tri-fold sheet, she scanned the photos from the gym, the beautifully healthy people working out on weight equipment, on spinning bikes, in kickboxing classes. The attendees in the yoga class all looked like models in their skin-tight clothing, and Liv wondered why they didn't use pictures of more out-of-shape, realistic people in their ads. Seemed like it would make more sense, draw in more clients if those pictured looked like they *needed* to be there. Isn't that why people joined a gym? Because they were out of shape and wanted to fix that? It was certainly Liv's reasoning.

On the back of the pamphlet, a name and number were stamped in cherry red. Julia Hastings. Liv figured each individual trainer had his or her own stamp and hit the back of the pamphlet before handing it out. Ms. Hastings came highly recommended by a couple of friends of Danny's. She was family, which was good. Liv wouldn't have to worry about awkwardly trying to answer the inevitable questions about her personal life. Most of all, Liv hoped Julia Hastings was gentle. Not necessarily in the exercise department, but in the encouragement department. She'd watched enough episodes of *The Biggest Loser* to know she would not do well being screamed at. More likely, if that was the method of training she was subjected to, she'd end up a blubbering glop of tears rocking in a corner. She'd have to make sure to tell Julia that right up front.

Her therapist, Peter, was not happy with this decision. He told Liv it was fine to join a gym if she simply wanted to improve her overall health and keep her heart in good working order. But enlisting a personal trainer and expecting to completely reshape her body was going to be an effort in futility—he was certain.

She'd been seeing him for nearly two years, so he knew her and her habits very well. He knew about her crappy self-esteem, that she was never happy with her own appearance and, therefore, was constantly trying to alter it.

He pursed his lips in thought when she talked about becoming a vegetarian. That lasted about a month and a half.

He propped his chin in his hand and stared at her when she told him she purchased the P90X workout system from an infomercial on TV and was going to get herself in shape, *finally*. She did it exactly twice.

He shook his head when she told him she signed herself up at an online fitness website and was keeping track of every calorie and every glass of water she consumed. It was three months since her last log-on.

Liv had been very excited to tell him about her new gym membership—a ridiculous $1200 for the year—and about all the information she was given regarding Julia Hastings. Of course, she'd been excited about every other physical fitness thing she signed on for as well. But this one was different. She was sure of it and she told Peter so.

"Why don't you just set yourself up for failure?" he asked pointedly.

"What do you mean?"

He was quiet for long moments, furrowing his brow, pressing his lips together. Finally, he asked, "Why do you constantly feel the need to change yourself?"

She simply blinked at him. Finally, truthfully, she answered. "I don't know."

"That's what we need to work on."

Peter was right. She knew that. Somewhere deep down in her being, she knew that. Why couldn't she just be happy with herself? With who she was? She was a good person inside, she knew that. Inside. Outside? That was the problem. Her reflection threw so much back at her and she had no idea why. Her hips were too wide, her hair was too dull, her eyes were too small, her tummy was too round, her skin was too pale, her ass was too large. There was always something to change. Always. Again, she knew deep down that this was not a healthy outlook, but she had no idea why she felt the way she did or how to fix it.

So she joined a gym. And tomorrow morning would be the first step in the, hopefully, not too long journey of Julia Hastings making her beautiful.

***

The next morning, Liv checked in at the gym's front desk filled with nervous anticipation. The atmosphere was what she'd hoped: energetic and exciting. The smell wasn't as awful as she'd feared: a little sweaty, but with a tinge of new plastic and leather. The pop of a racquetball hitting the wall and bouncing back to its server seemed almost cheerful to her, and she peeked through the Plexiglas wall to the court one floor below. Doing her level best, she willed herself not to be intimidated by the buzz of liveliness or the sheer volume of people, all panting and perspiring at seven a.m.

Liv had never joined a gym before, but this one came with a big, gay thumbs up. Danny and all his friends worked out here. So did many of the lesbians she knew.

And don't know, she thought, as a woman with short, dark hair and the body of a professional athlete passed by and smiled, setting off Liv's gaydar.

The gym was located downtown and was easily accessible from half a dozen office buildings, several bars and restaurants, and the museum. Because of that, Danny said it didn't have a ton of down time and was almost always at least half-full. Liv wondered if maybe she'd meet some new people.

"Olivia Keegan?" Liv was pulled back to the moment by an affable-looking woman. Her blonde hair was short and tucked behind her ears, and her brown eyes held warmth and gentleness. "I'm Julia Hastings," she said as she held out her hand.

"Liv. Please." Liv shook the hand firmly. "It's nice to meet you."

"Come with me to my office and we'll talk about what you're hoping to accomplish here."

The first thing that struck Liv as they walked was that Julia wasn't a twig. She was by no means overweight or even a little chubby, but she was not painfully skinny. Liv liked that. A lot. Julia was obviously toned and femininely muscular, but she had curves—round hips, ample breasts, and a tummy that was not flat. Somehow, those characteristics made her seem more real to Liv, more human, and would go a long way in helping her follow Julia's guidelines.

Julia's office was more like a shared closet, small to the point of being claustrophobic and made even more so by the second body seated at the other desk. Thankfully, that second body excused himself and left them the room, such as it was. Liv thanked her lucky stars she wasn't any bigger as she shimmied sideways and plopped into the plastic chair that seemed like the room must have been built around.

"It's a little small in here," Julia said, apology in her voice.

"Yeah, way to make people feel like they *need* to join a gym."

Julia laughed, a deeper sound than Liv expected. "You figured out our dastardly plan."

Danny was right; she was instantly comfortable with Julia. Even when the questions got a bit personal or embarrassing, like admitting the number of times per week that she exercised was actually zero. Even when Julia asked her to step on the scale. Even when they sat down to go over all the results and possible solutions. She never once felt judged or scolded or condescended to. Julia was funny, gentle, and kind. Shockingly, Liv found herself not depressed over the information they'd come up with, but rather, excited to get started on some sort of program.

"Now," Julia said, setting aside computer printouts and red pen, "this is where I get to play a little bit of psychologist."

"Okay," Liv drew out, her eyebrows almost meeting above her nose.

"The first thing I want you to do is ease up on yourself."

Liv blinked at her.

"What's going on at home?"

"What do you mean?"

Julia sat forward, her elbows on the desk, and looked Liv in the eye. "The majority of women like you who come to me—who have never seen the inside of a gym in their lives—usually have had something happen to give them a kick. Class reunion is coming up, they got dumped, their significant other is cheating on them..." Something on Liv's face must have given her away because Julia stopped there. "Is that it? Your girlfriend cheated on you?"

Liv was too mortified by the tears that pooled in her eyes to take a moment and wonder how Julia knew her sexual preference—though it made sense that Danny probably spilled the beans. She gazed down at her hands in her lap, but Julia ducked her head to recapture Liv's eyes.

"Hey," Julia said, her voice a bit sharper. When Liv looked up, she continued. "Screw her. You're tough on yourself. I can see it. And I bet she's made you that way. So you listen to me right now: you are *not* in terrible shape. You are *not* overweight. You are *not* unattractive. I want you to put all of that out of your head right now. Just because—what's her name?"

"Diane."

"Just because Diane was stupid enough to let you go doesn't mean there's anything wrong with you. You need to understand that and accept it. There is no judgment coming from me, and I don't want there to be any from you either. You are a beautiful person. Now let's make you into a *physically fit*, beautiful person. What do you say?"

Liv nodded, not trusting her own voice. She pressed her lips together and went back to studying her hands in her lap while she fumbled to regain her composure. When she finally looked back up at Julia, the silent question must have been more obvious than she thought because Julia smiled at her and said, "I've been doing this for a long time and like I said, I get a lot of women in here like you. I've gotten to the point where I can read you all like books. We're so hard on ourselves, us women. You know? The media says we need to be thinner, thinner, thinner, and our significant others can sometimes make us feel like we need to be more like what the media says, and frankly, the look the media touts is pretty much impossible for all but a really small percentage of us to reach. So…we're working on a futile task, like washing a floor that we'll never finish or shopping for groceries from a list that will never end. It's so unfair." She stopped, took a deep breath, looked at Liv for a long moment. "My goal is to teach every woman that comes to me unhappy with her body how to be not only physically fit, but mentally fit…to accept who she is and to love herself for that. We're all beautiful."

"We're kind of stubborn," Liv pointed out, her voice throaty.

"I didn't say it was an easy goal." Julia laughed that deep sound again and in that moment, Liv knew this was going to be different.

"So?" Julia repeated her earlier question. "What do you say? Are you ready to get started?"

Liv gave one determined nod. "I am."

"Great. Follow me."

For the next hour, Julia escorted Liv through the gym, showed her how to work various equipment, talked about the benefits of each one. They peeked in at the racquetball courts, Liv briefly wondering if she'd ever feel confident enough to play, thinking that hitting the ball against the wall all by herself actually looked like it might be fun. There was a pool, a regular gym in which basketball games were played, among other things. The yoga room was filled with spandex-clad women twisted like pretzels and Liv almost laughed out loud when she tried to picture herself attempting any of the moves. Another room contained a kickboxing class—"Great for taking out your frustrations!" Julia informed her—and still another held a spinning class with thirty-five people pedaling bikes to nowhere. But the music was pumpingly energetic and Liv stopped to watch, tickled by a tiny desire to maybe give it a try.

"It's more fun than you might think," Julia said, standing close. "And you can burn a ton of calories once you get going."

Liv nodded, and her head kept bobbing to the beat of the song, a popular dance mix she loved.

By the time they finished with the tour and overall instructions and gone over Julia's proposed exercise plan for her, Liv was utterly pumped.

"I don't think I can leave without doing something," she said, her grin wide. "I want to start on the treadmill. Can I do that? Is that dumb?"

Julia's expression was that of a teacher's pride in her favorite student. "No physical activity is dumb. Come on. I'll get you all set up."

Forty-five minutes worth of brisk walking later (and an episode and a half of *Friends*), sweating, heart pumping like crazy, Liv felt more alive and energetic than she had in—she couldn't remember when. There was a skip in her step as she crossed the parking lot to her car, again feeling that this was a step for her, that this was going to be different. She felt almost reborn, like she was a new person—or would be once she got herself on a schedule and into a habit. Maybe this was the change she'd been needing for so long. She could almost see Peter rolling his eyes at her, but she didn't care, because she also felt excited anticipation rather than paralyzing fear about meeting up with Dorian Garrison later.

Oh, yeah. This was going to change her life.

THE FITNESS INSTRUCTOR

When Julia Hastings first began her career as a fitness instructor, women like Olivia Keegan used to piss her off. She'd get so annoyed with the whining, the self-doubt, the oh-I'm-so-fat-woe-is-me crap, it was all she could do to keep from screaming at them to suck it up and stop the blubbering, to shout in their faces, "Nobody can make you feel crummy about yourself but you! So cut it out!" She'd finish with an appointment, retreat to her tiny office, and drop her forehead onto her desk with a tooth-clattering thump and a frustrated groan.

Julia was only twenty-five then and certainly hadn't seen enough life at that point to have any clue how a woman's mind worked.

As she got older and dealt with more female clients, she learned to accept them for who they were and she tried to steer them—as gently as possible—in the right direction as far as how they looked at themselves in the mirror. It was not an easy task at all. The things she said to Liv were all true. The media was not only unhelpful, it was alarmingly harmful. TV shows and movies and magazines all told women they weren't skinny enough, they weren't pretty enough, they weren't tan enough, change your hair color, change your eye color, pay for fake nails and fake eyelashes and fake hair, for extensions and fake boobs. Julia did not envy anybody trying to raise a teenage girl in this day and age. Healthy self-esteem seemed next to impossible to grasp, and Julia learned quickly that sympathy was sorely needed as she did her best to guide her female clients toward confidence. Not at all an easy feat, what with the media and society and men all working against her.

Self-confidence. That was the key to a healthy outlook on life. Hell, it was the key to actually *enjoying* life, at least in Julia's opinion. If she could get a woman to be confident in herself, there was nothing she couldn't do. Julia told her clients that all the time. Confidence in a woman was damn sexy.

After all, that's how she'd first been drawn to Christine.

A scoff escaped her lips as she thought about how funny it was—except not really—that something initially so awesome and wonderful could do a complete one-eighty and bite you right in the ass. How ironic that it was Christine's self-confidence that sent Julia's right into the crapper. Here she spent her working hours doing her best to help women feel better about themselves…if they only knew she barely had the ability to help herself anymore.

But thank god for my job, she thought, heading to the spinning room. The fact that it was physical helped a great deal. Even if her brain had become crippled by worry and doubt, her muscles stayed hard and toned. In order to take up more time, she picked up extra classes, and covered for her coworkers who needed time off. She was especially fond of teaching the spinning classes because the blasting, pumping music was perfect for shutting the maddeningly circular thoughts out of her head, at least for fifty minutes. And fifty minutes was better than nothing. So she donned the microphone, plugged in her iPod, chose a wickedly fast-paced playlist, and drove the crap out of the class—and herself—for nearly an hour. When it was over and the last attendee dragged his sweaty ass out the door on rubbery legs, Julia took her time wiping down her bike, as her own quads trembled from the exertion of the class.

"Wow. Who pissed in your Wheaties this morning?" Tommy T stood in the doorway leaning on the doorjamb, arms folded across his chest, and looking like a Greek sculpture. His last name was Polish and virtually unpronounceable, so he'd simply become Tommy T.

"What do you mean?"

"Come on, Jules. How long have we known each other?" He was right. Tommy probably knew her better than almost anybody; they'd been coworkers and friends for more than a decade. He was her confidante and he gave surprisingly good advice for a straight man who looked like an Adonis and had a name that should belong to a porn star. He walked into the room and ducked his head, trying to catch her eye. She avoided his gaze, afraid he'd see right into her head. "You just about killed your class. What's going on?"

"Nothing. I'm fine." Julia mopped the perspiration from her forehead and glanced at Tommy, then made a show of gathering her things.

"Uh-huh," Tommy said. "I'm sure I don't have to tell you that I don't believe you."

Julia sidled by him. "I'm fine, T."

She could feel Tommy's eyes on her as she headed down the hall. "You know where to find me when you're ready to talk about it," he called after her.

Hating the feeling of running away, despite the fact that it was exactly what she was doing, Julia found peace in the staff restroom where she stripped down and stepped into the shower, and prayed for the water to wash away the stress that seemed to be closing in on her.

Why now? That was the question foremost in her mind. She'd been dealing with the whole Christine situation for months now. No, more than a year, if she was going to be honest with herself. More than two years, really. Okay, three. She'd been dealing with it for three years. And those were only the dalliances she knew about as fact. Maybe Christine had been cheating on her from the very beginning.

Julia closed her eyes and set her forehead against the tile wall of the shower while the water pounded her shoulder blades. Twelve years? Was it possible Christine was unfaithful for all that time? But why? She seemed happy, as happy as Julia when they first committed to each other, first moved in together, toasted with very expensive champagne when Christine opened her law firm. Julia was there for every momentous occasion in Christine's career. Happily. Supportively.

Faithfully.

The first one to raise Julia's hackles was a client of Christine's. The husband owned a trio of auto repair shops and thought Christine walked on water. If only he'd known Christine's fingers did the walking all over his beautiful wife. Julia had popped by the office to surprise Christine with lunch and waited patiently in the lobby for her to finish up a meeting with the couple. When the group of them came out, there was something—*something*—about the way Christine looked at the wife, the way she kept her hand at the small of the woman's back, gently directing her, the way the wife gazed up into Christine's eyes. Julia knew that look. She'd had it on her own face. She knew the charm Christine could project, the way she could make you feel like there was nobody else in the room. That's how the wife looked at her that day: like Julia had when she'd first become enamored with Christine. The husband was oblivious then. Probably still was. Men tended to be naïve that way, Julia knew, never thinking another woman might peak the sexual interest of his wife.

Julia never said a thing to Christine. To this day, she wasn't sure why. She simply watched and waited and before she could decide what to do, it was over. The whole thing played itself out in about three months. The late nights "at work" stopped. Christine seemed much more present, much less removed, than she had been since she'd taken the couple on as clients. She bought Julia a gorgeous pair of diamond earrings. Julia took them as an unspoken apology and decided to just let it go.

That was the first one.

Six months went by before number two came along.

With a frustrated sigh, Julia changed into clean clothes, knowing she had some paperwork to finish up before she met with her next new client. In her tiny cubby—it was just too small to refer to it as an office—she turned the framed photo of a grinning Christine to face away from her, plugged her ear buds into her ears and hoped to blast the thoughts of her crumbling relationship out of her head, just as she had with the spin class. The lyrics of Sara Bareilles were just too poignant for her mood, so she scanned for something with a good beat and shallow, meaningless words, settling on a Britney Spears tune.

The paperwork killed a half hour. Back-to-back clients took over another two hours. Two men this time, a happy surprise since the majority of her clients were women. The first one was a walking stereotype, a large guy who was certain he knew more about the equipment and proper weight-lifting procedures than Julia did, and took great pleasure in finishing her sentences. Not to mention, he never looked above her breasts when she spoke to him. When she finally finished with him, she momentarily wondered if she could squeeze in another quick shower, just to wash off the unpleasantness he'd left crawling on her skin. The second client was a nice guy, middle-aged and determined to get himself into some kind of reasonable shape. He wasn't a lost cause and Julia spent much of their time convincing him of this fact. He was a quick study and she predicted he would be one of those few people who actually got his money's worth out of his gym membership by returning on a regular basis.

Lunch consisted of some yogurt mixed with granola she'd made herself last night. Julia wasn't one of those fitness instructors who lived on rabbit food; she usually had a hearty sandwich—healthy, but hearty—packed along with several snacks, but lately she'd seemed to have misplaced her appetite. Strategically avoiding Tommy, who shot her a knowing look from across the row of treadmills as she scurried past, she ate quickly and headed for the Body Pump class she taught three times a week.

Early afternoon classes pulled in a completely different crowd than early morning or five o'clock. Entering the room, she quickly counted nine people, six of whom were regulars, two who she thought were completely new, and one she'd seen around the gym, but never in this particular class. Body Pump wasn't nearly as mindless as spinning, but Julia enjoyed it. Pumping music added an element of fun to what was essentially a basic weight-lifting routine. Strolling the room and helping her attendees learn to do the moves correctly, learn what would best help them tone whichever muscle group they were on was especially rewarding. What made it all worthwhile for Julia was seeing somebody's face when that person finally "got it," felt the right burn, or even realized he or she needed to move to a heavier weight. It was a big part of why she entered the fitness industry in the first place. Her younger, naïve self wanted to shape up the entire planet. Her older, realistic self was simply happy to help a handful of people a day.

She also liked the Body Pump class because, when she wasn't helping a student, she could focus on her own body, her own breathing, the working of her own muscle groups as she lifted and pushed and strained. A good muscle workout always made her head feel better.

Once class was over, however, her brain went right back to its turbulence, spinning and tossing, not giving her a moment's rest. She took a load of towels to the laundry room and threw them in, refilled her water bottle from the fountain in the hall, and ensconced herself behind her desk once more, hoping to focus on more paperwork. Or maybe shoot herself in the head.

The backwards frame caught her eye and she felt the sudden, unbearable urge to hear Christine's voice, to be on the receiving end of some reassurance, to feel like she was just having a weird mood and everything would be okay if she just hung in there. Before she could talk herself out of it, she'd picked up the phone and dialed her partner's cell phone number.

When voicemail picked up, Julia replaced the handset more roughly than necessary. Then she picked it back up and dialed the office number. After a brief conversation, she replaced the handset again and sat staring at the phone. She muttered, "That was weird," just as her office door clicked shut.

"What was weird?" Tommy T stood against the closed door. His bulk took up the majority of any extra space and made Julia feel like she was sitting in an elevator.

"I just called Christine's office."

"Didn't get her, I bet." Tommy tried not to scowl. He was unsuccessful.

"No, but I got Bertie. She never answers Christine's line. She said Jenna quit this week."

"Jenna, the little hussy Christine was banging?"

"That's the one," Julia replied, and her expression perfectly combined a grimace and a sneer.

"Good riddance."

"I know. I'm just surprised Christine didn't say anything."

Tommy scoffed. "I'm surprised you still expect her to tell you things."

Julia shook her head in self-deprecation. "I know. I know. I can't seem to help it."

Despite his size and the lack of space in the room, Tommy squatted down to look his friend in the eye. "Jules, honey, you deserve so much better." His voice was gentle and kind. He closed a hand the size of a catcher's mitt over hers. "How much longer are you going to take this?"

Her eyes filled, but as soon as she felt the tears, Julia got angry. "Damn her for making me feel like this," she said hoarsely. "Damn her." The tears spilled over. "Damn her."

"I know," Tommy said with a nod. He shifted to his knees next to her so he could wrap her in his embrace. She continued to curse her partner even as she buried her face in Tommy's shoulder and cried.

"I don't understand," she said, her voice muffled in his shirt. "I do everything for her. I love her so much. Why does she hurt me?"

Tommy rocked her for long moments, murmured in her ear, promised her it would all work out for the best, that she just needed to put herself first for a change. They were the same things he'd been saying to her for almost three years now, and they usually rolled over her and then right off onto the ground and she went on with business as usual. But today was different. She had no idea why, but for some reason, this time she heard him, heard his words, heard his worry for her, his anger for her, his frustration with her. She heard it all loud and clear and knew it was time.

Time to do something about it.

Julia sat back in her chair, away from Tommy, wiped her hand over her face, reached for a tissue. "You're right," she said simply.

Tommy blinked at her. "I'm sorry, but...what?"

One corner of her mouth quirked up. "You heard me."

"I did. I just needed to be sure. I don't think you've ever said those words to me before."

"Hardy har har."

His face softened. "I'm right about what?" he asked gently.

Julia blew out a breath, cleared her throat. "I don't deserve this. I'm a good wife. I'm a supportive partner. I do my best for her, and she should treat me with respect, not run off and fuck every pretty girl that walks into her office." She said the last line with more malice than she'd expected to, and Tommy chuckled.

"You're preaching to the choir, babe," he said. "But I'm glad to hear it."

"It's time to face the music. Isn't it?" Her voice was small again.

"Has been for a while now."

She nodded once. "It has." A glance at the clock told her it was just after three. "I suddenly realized I have a long overdue appointment with a lawyer. Mind if I cut out a little early?"

He shook his head and stood. "Go for it."

Julia held Tommy's gaze for a moment, and her heart filled to bursting with gratitude. "Thank you," she said in a near-whisper. She stepped forward and wrapped her arms around his huge neck, feeling the muscles ripple in his shoulders. He hugged her back tightly.

"You're welcome. Call me and let me know how you are, okay?"

"Okay."

He released her, but held her shoulders and looked her in the eye. "Promise me."

"I promise."

"Good luck, Jules."

Less than a half hour later, Julia pulled her car into a parking spot in the lot for Davis and Fichter, Attorneys. Christine's convertible, cherry-red BMW sat in her usual reserved spot and for a second, Julia's palms began to sweat. She quickly shook off the fear and steeled herself as she got out of the car. She had every right to confront this situation. She was doing nothing wrong. Not a thing. Repeating it in her head like a mantra, she entered the lobby and smiled at Bertie. A perverse sense of pleasure flooded her at the site of Jenna's now-empty space.

"Hi, Bertie. Is Christine in?"

"Hey, Jules, how are you?" Bertie seemed genuinely happy to see her; she was the one person in this office that Julia thought was authentic, who pulled no punches and played no roles.

"I'm okay, Bertie. How about you?"

"It's better than the alternative, right?" They both laughed and Bertie continued with, "Christine's got a client in with her right now, but they should be finishing up soon."

"Good. I'll wait." She stepped to the chairs in the waiting area and glimpsed through the magazines.

"Can I get you anything?" Bertie asked.

"Oh, no, I'm good. Thank you, though."

As Julia chose a *People* from three months ago and sat, a tall, leggy, gorgeous blonde walked through the lobby and smiled at her with too-white teeth. She was beautiful, but in a nothing-on-this-body-is-natural sort of way. Julia's eyes followed her to the end of the hall where she entered Christine's office and closed the door behind her.

"Who was that?" she asked Bertie before she could stop herself.

"New intern. Kerry—."

"—Kerry." They said her name in unison and then their eyes met. "Yeah, I've heard all about her," Julia said, trying and failing to keep the disdain from her tone. "You like her?"

Bertie grimaced, searching for the right words. "She's…an acquired taste."

"I'll bet."

The switchboard rang, stealing Bertie from her, so Julia returned to her magazine. She pretended to read, but her mind was on Kerry the Intern. Julia couldn't put her finger on why, but there was not a doubt in her mind that Kerry the Intern already was one of Christine's conquests. When Christine's door opened and people filed out, Julia's suspicions were solidified. Kerry looked at Christine with unadulterated lust, and walked much too closely to her. Christine ate it up, and there was the hand on the small of the back again.

The second she saw Julia, however, she took a quick step away and put more space between them. Their eyes met and Julia knew that Christine knew and she was glad for it. Less explanation for her to give.

"Hi, sweetie," Christine said, her voice too sweet. She bent to kiss Julia's cheek. "What are you doing here?" She introduced Julia as her wife to the three clients on their way out as well as to Kerry the Intern, who paled noticeably. Julia barely kept her grin hidden.

"I need to talk to you," Julia said simply as hands were shaken and goodbyes were said. The clients left and Kerry the Intern hovered for only a split second before she bee-lined for anyplace else.

"Oh, honey. I'm really swamped," Christine began. "Can't it wait until I get—."

"No." Julia was not the kind of person who often interrupted, but this time, she felt justified. "No, it cannot wait. We need to talk. Now. Right now."

She turned on her heel and headed down the hall towards Christine's office, chin up, heart pounding, leaving her soon-to-be ex-wife blinking in astonished confusion behind her.

By Georgia Beers

Novels

Finding Home
Mine
Fresh Tracks
Too Close to Touch
Thy Neighbor's Wife
Turning the Page
96 Hours
Slices of Life

Anthologies

Outsiders

Georgia Beers
www.georgiabeers.com